A Place We All Know

A Collection of Short Stories

by

Kevin Winter

Hilltop Publishing & Designs

For more information, contact Hilltop Publishing & Designs, 5830B Highway 72, Walnut, MS 38683 or visit *http://www.facebook.com/kevinwinterwrites*.

ISBN: 153081894X
ISBN-13: 978-1530818945

For my Haley.
They're all for you.

Except for the one about the zombies.
That one was definitely for me.

Table of Contents

A Place We All Know
An Invitation

"Why did you and your wife move back home?"
I turned around and pointed at myself.
"Uhhh, me?"
"Yeah," she said. "What *possessed* y'all to come back *here*?"

From an objective point of view, it was a good question.

Our previous place of residence was, indeed, quite nice. We owned a large comfortable house with plenty of room for us, kids (we had one at the time and several more planned), and pets. It was well located, convenient to shopping, dining, and entertainment. The schools were a little larger and more crowded than I personally prefer but had achieved extremely high ratings. My workplace was within a reasonable commute. Haley had several close friends in the area and had become involved in a monthly book club and bunco group. We had everything we needed and were within an arm's reach of everything else.

During our time there, I acted on my childhood dream of writing a novel and completed the project over the course of a year.

My plan was simple and I was diligently adherent to it. I would write no less than one chapter each month. When the words were flowing and the plot points easy to maneuver, I would write two. During these exceptionally productive months, I would also churn out a short story or two once my novel quota had been met. Although the entire affair of following a protagonist through a book's worth of action, introducing and closing ancillary arcs, and making the whole thing readable and engaging was a mental challenge, I greatly enjoyed the experience and learned more about writing and my own voice than any tutorial or self-help book could ever teach me.

At the end of the twelve month period, I forced myself to pause and reflect on what I had created. My novel recounted a story that was of the dark and twisty variety, the first in a saga involving a uniquely loyal hitman's entanglement in a crime syndicate takeover. The prose was blunt and edgy, the characters relatively fleshy and deliciously unpredictable. The chapters were a good length and contained a healthy mix of cliffhangers and closures. From my utterly biased opinion, it was a good work and I remain proud of it. However, there was a missing ingredient, something that held it back from being truly great. As you can imagine, I spent many sleepless nights tumbling it over and over in my mind, searching for that missing piece.

Meanwhile, I also took inventory of the short fiction that had arisen from the year prior. Some were complete and polished (many, such as *What the Storm Did* and *A Sunset for a Suicidist* were already published in various outlets of short fiction) while others were mere outlines or rough drafts or the first few paragraphs of a concept I needed to get out of my mind. *Me and Miss Rosie*, for instance, was one of the latter. As I read back through these bits and fragments, I began to realize something, something that should have been immediately evident, but that required a step back for me to see. These stories, small or incomplete though they were, all had two things in common. Firstly, I cared more about the characters therein - their struggles and successes, where they came from, where they were going, the choices they made along the way - than I did for those in my novel. And, secondly, they all had their roots planted in the same fertile soil. The same *place*.

The missing ingredient. At last, I had found it.

Place.

My novel, for all its merits, is a flawed work. I can admit that. Now, as a side note, I shamelessly hope that one day it will be read and enjoyed by people outside of my network of first-passers, therefore I will not completely disparage it here. However, for me to declare it as anything but flawed would not be an honest and true assessment. Its imperfection is its setting - a fictional place called The City - and, more precisely, its author's unfamiliarity with it. I have visited metropolitan areas, have friends that have lived in them to varying degrees of satisfaction, but I don't *know* The City. If I close my eyes, I can't effectively build it around me, set it correctly into motion. I lack the proper building blocks and the knowledge of its rhythm and pace. Someday, I may gain these, but for now, they remain foreign to me.

Hickahala County, on the other hand, is like home. It *is* home, in fact, or at least my mental composite of it. Although no less fictitious than The City, it felt more real to me and stirred a more solid emotional attachment between myself and the people on the page. I believe you will have a similar experience, whether you grew up in Chicago or Cleveland or California or the Carolinas, because no matter where it may be, home is a remarkably universal construct. Even though our own version of it may go by different names and be populated with different faces, it is a place we all know. It is, as Mr. Mac would put it in *The Traveler*, the best place.

And it is to this place, I now invite you.

The stories that follow have now been completed and shined. Read and edited, reread and reedited. The work came with relatively little effort, driven by the same spirit that had possessed me to move my family away from the convenience of our comfortable suburbanite existence and back to the home we adore. I was compelled to complete these characters' journeys and present them to you. I couldn't not. And now, I cannot wait for you to look through the windows I have created into their lives.

But first, a note and some thanks.

To those from *my* real-life home - Don't try too hard to connect the characters herein to any actual folks around town. In some instances, I have allowed the actual to influence and color my imagination, but each of these characters - good, bad, and indifferent - are much more me than anyone else. As much as I desire for you to feel this journey as real, keep in mind that, with the exception of *A Young Man, Once*, it is make-believe. There are no ulterior motives or hidden messages here. So save yourself the trouble and try not thinking too hard.

And now the thanks. There are too many of my first-pass readers to thank each by name. You know who you are. Thank you for being flexible and honest. Whether I sent you the wildly imaginative *From the Backs of Four Shop-Rite* Bags or the grounded *Me and Miss* Rosie, you rolled with me. I hope that as you read through these stories again (or for the umpteenth time), you will enjoy them as much as you (hopefully) did the first time around and that you know that without your contributions, they would never be here before you. To my family, friends, and neighbors - thanks to you for being those things to us. Your love for us helps us through each day and is a commodity too valuable to ignore. Haley and I are truly blessed and we owe each of you our gratitude. And to Haley - it seems too simple to say thank you to the one for whom these stories were written in the first place. You allow me to dream and yet, you somehow manage to keep me on track. You are my sounding board, my first and last reader. If you like it, that is all I need.

So, why *had* we decided to move back home?

I answered with a question of my own. "How could we not? There are a million nice places in the world, but there'll always only be one home."

Now, without further adieu, come along with me. There's no need in bringing anything. Leave all your baggage, care, and worries behind. As my mother is fond of saying, all you need is you. We're going to a place we all know, every last one of us. A place where you can sit back, relax, and enjoy the pie.

Welcome home.

Kevin Winter

Walnut, Mississippi 2016

Me and Miss Rosie

one

I'll never forget the day I met her.

It was a Sunday.

I had just the previous day unpacked the majority of the essential boxes, folded them down, and stacked them neatly on the old busted curb for pick-up. The bedroom was set up. Clothes were hanging in the master closet and of course the bathroom things were splayed out neatly on the vanity in places that felt comfortable. Despite the fact that some serious work was required in the kitchen and that the upstairs room above the garage was stacked high with duct-taped boxes filled with books and pictures and videos and candles and everything else that could wait, all in all when I dozed off that first night, I didn't feel as if I was moving. It would be untruthful for me to say that I was filled up with a sense of being completely at home or even quite settled in, but I will venture so far as to say that for the first time in a while, I felt stationary. As if I were in a place I could stay and, if I were to stay, I might eventually come to call home.

That was Saturday. Sunday was when it would all begin.

The congregation was small, only about fifty or so, and I had the back pew all to myself until just after the close of the first hymn when a young mother and her curly-headed daughter slipped past me and sat down. Throughout the service, their matching curious blue eyes ran me over. I'd look over periodically and smile and nod, but they just kept on looking as if they could smell the city in my clothes. I half expected for someone, the robust rosy-cheeked songleader or the hunkered down bifocaled elder or the mustached podium-gripping preacher to point me out and politely demand that I stand and introduce myself. But they didn't. I know they saw me and marked my presence however, like snipers picking out a target that was worth a bit of patience.

It was hot in the church building and I expected no less for a sunny July midmorning in the great Hospitality State. Everyone was sweating. In the quiet interlude between songs, all that could be heard was the flapping of hand-fans and the soft cooing of infants; markedly absent was the electrical buzz of central air conditioning. But down front, on the very first pew, there sat a shrunken red-headed old lady wearing a padded navy blazer and a shawl and her legs were covered over by a thick knitted afghan. Moreover, she was cross-armed and clutching herself as if we were not indoors in sweltering Hickahala County, Mississippi, but rather out in the frigidity of a nor'eastern. I smiled and wiped the moisture from my forehead before it dripped down my nose. Then I nodded to the mother sitting wide-eyed beside me, tried to appear uninteresting, and waited for the service to end.

After the closing prayer, I bent and grabbed up my leatherbound Bible and turned toward the door and there stood Nora Jo with her hand flopped out for a shake. And she just started talking.

"Hi there," she drawled. "My given name is Nora Jo, but just about everybody 'round here calls me Preacher's Wife cuz, you guessed it ding-ding-ding, I'm married to the preacher." Then she laughed for too long and waved a hand in front of her face. I smiled and gave my own name as I shook her dead fish of a hand. "Oh, so you're that airline pilot that has moved into the Bakers' old place. Well, welcome to Millwood Branch and we hope you like it here and if you need anything don't you hesitate to call on Gene and me, we'd just love to help."

It was my second day in town and I had met no one. I had made no passing mention of my occupation in the service station or the local grocery store or the corner barber shop. My realtor operated out of Memphis and had no connection to the folks way out here in Millwood Branch. I guess it could have been the bumper sticker on my KIA that read **I'd rather be flying**, but I doubt it. People in the country just tend to know things. Once you get out to where the air is clear and the stars are bright, information, transmitted hither and thither via the oft-beguiled conduits of country gossip, becomes as ubiquitous as the kudzu.

I thanked her kindly and took a step around her and into the flow of people making their way to the propped open double doors. Everyone smiled in that way that is exclusive to southern small-towners and I tried to smile back in the same blessed way as I folded the Bible against my chest as a shield against lengthy conversations. I was almost to the doors when she called out again.

"Mr. Johnston!" Nora Jo Preacher's Wife shouted. "Oh Mr. Johnston, I almost nearly forgot."

I turned and there she was again, grinning like a possum eating the unmentionable.

"I was going to introduce you to Miss Rosie, Mr. Johnston, and I came near to forgetting. Come on." Then she clutched my arm with a grip that I couldn't imagine ever likening to a dead fish and brought me through the small crowd and out into the sunshine. I squinted against the sky from above and the sheen reflecting up from the white gravel parking area from below and by the time my eyes adjusted to the light, we were approaching Gene, the preacher, and the little red-headed lady from the front pew. She was shaking his hand as old ladies do and shaking her head to match.

"Not your best, Preacher, I can tell you that," she was saying. "And I'll tell you something else, too. If somebody don't turn down that cool air I reckon I'll move membership to the congregation down in Martin or Littleton or someplace else. Move my weekly tithe, too, I will. It's cold enough to slaughter hogs in there."

Just then, the preacher looked up and seeing us, his face went slack with relief. He stabbed his hand in my direction and introduced himself with the title of Brother. I shook it with what I hoped would pass for a firm country grip and traded names with the preacher.

"And this," said Nora Jo, thrusting me at the little old lady, "is Miss Rosie Cotcher, our most tenured Sunday School teacher and pillar of the Millwood Branch community." The old lady's lip quivered before pulling back into a snarl, an actual snarl, revealing a pearly set of dentures stuck with flecks of lipstick, the shade of which I would place somewhere between red-red and ultra-red. "Rosie, meet Mr. Johnston."

She looked me up and down as if I were a bunch of bananas at the market. Then she held out her hand which was all knuckles and blue veins for me to shake. "Nice to know you, Mr. Johnston. I trust Nora Jo here will parade you about until you've met everyone."

Nora Jo laughed and waved that hand in front of her face as if it were on fire. "Ding-ding-ding. You got me. I love my fellowship." At length, the laughing and waving stopped. "Mr. Johnston comes to us out of Memphis, Miss Rosie. He's moved into the Bakers' house right in the slap-dab middle of town."

"How come you moved out here from the big city?" Miss Rosie inquired. Her tone was suspicious enough for the question to pass for the opening of an interrogation.

I told her that over time, big cities can start to feel mighty small and cramped and that I needed to loosen my belt and stretch my legs and catch my breath and that this town felt like the right place in which to do so.

"Huh," she said, apparently pleased with the answer. "And your job? Have you found work to suit you out here in the sticks?"

"Why, Rosie," said Nora Jo, "haven't you heard? Mr. Johnston here is a commercial airplane pilot for Gulf Coastal Airline." Only she pronounced the word as "arrow-plane", at which normally I would roll my eyes, but on this occasion, without reason, I found cute and endearing.

I explained that it was true. I was a pilot and I was simply commuting the hour to and from Memphis International Airport three times a week for flights. And her face changed. The sourness evaporated, leaving behind the hint of a grin on the face of an elderly woman that could bear the label of sweet. "A pilot?" she said slowly, before a sharp inward breath and her continuance. "Do you like caramel pie, Mr. Johnston? If you don't, you'd be a fool."

I told her that caramel was a personal favorite of mine, just behind pecan in the pie pecking order. The preacher and his wife giggled at this, reminding me that they were still there, hovering.

"Third house down Bullfrog Road, just past the silo. I'll have pie and coffee but I'm not feeding you a full meal so you'd better come with something solid already in your belly. Thursday evening, if your schedule allows, Friday if not."

Thursday, I said, would do just fine and I'd bring a moderately full stomach and a sweet tooth.

Then she nodded her head and crunched her way through the white glaring gravel to a boat of a Chrysler and drove away. The preacher's eyebrows were wrinkled halfway up his forehead and it took even Nora Jo a moment to catch her tongue.

"Well, ding-ding-ding. She sure does like you."

two

There's nothing wetter than a rain shower in the South.

The air had grown thicker as the week progressed, although if you'd asked me on Sunday afternoon I would have laughed and called it impossible. The weathermen out of Memphis, each with his or her own flare of flamboyancy and exaggeration, paced in front of red topographical maps of the Mid-South viewing area and stressed the import of heat indices, that deadly combo-pack of temperature and humidity. In a few months it would be hurricanes. Then the blizzards, wind chill, falling chunks of ice the size of nickels, golf balls, or even grapefruits. Then the pollen. And finally back around to that booger they just couldn't seem to flick, the heat. Usually, I'd just smirk at them and wait for the seven day planner but that week it was difficult to ignore the moisture in the air and the intense blare of the sun what with the never-ceasing chugga-chugga-chugga of the age old air conditioning unit I'd inherited from the Bakers and the mountain of unwashed sweat-soaked pilot shirts in my closet floor. Something had to give and late that Wednesday night, something gave. A front swept over the Chickasaw Bluffs and finally the water began falling in drops rather than hanging about in a suffocating vapor.

I had spent the majority of that Thursday setting up my office as the rain drummed on the roof overhead like countless tiny fingers and ran like the Mighty Mississip' from the drainpipe at the corner of the house to the edge of the yard and down through the grate set into my side of North Main Street. Earlier that week, I had made my scheduled flights to Atlanta and New Orleans plus I had tacked on a red eye to Miami in repayment to a pilot friend for filling in for me during the rough patch around the time Tiffany and I made our break. Therefore, I had accomplished precious little on the house. But with the rain came a deepened resolve to empty still more of the cardboard boxes and, excepting an abbreviated turkey-on-toasted-white break at noon, I worked straight through the day and by half-past four o'clock that afternoon, I had laid out a workable and quite organized little office in the front cubby of the Baker House, even by my own slightly compulsive standards.

My stomach gurgled emptily as I surveyed the smallish room now precisely arranged with my dark oak desk and hutch, dueling bookcases, one lined with flight manuals and catalogues and the other with Faulkner, Welty, O'Conner, and even two of Grisham's earlier works that Tiff had bought for me, and the floor lamp standing tall in the corner. I was reminded of the mediocrity of my hasty lunch as well as Rosie Cotcher's stern instructions to see to the primary source of my nourishment prior to our dessert engagement that evening. And so as the rain continued to cascade down in sheets, I microwaved a plateful of chicken and cheese mexican rolls, blew cool air onto them until struck with the light-headedness of near-hyperventilation, and gobbled them up. Then I traded my jogging shorts and grimy tank-top for a clean pair of khakis and the most unwrinkled golf shirt I could locate, backed my KIA out of the garage and into the downpour, and set off in search of Bullfrog Road.

I missed the turn off of Highway 354 on the first pass and had to turn around in someone's muddy driveway and very nearly got mired down and stuck before the front wheels finally caught and reversed me back out onto the pavement. I missed the turn for a number of reasons, the near-blinding rain being chief among them. Others included the fact that 354 wound back and forth on top of itself like a river creating oxbows for no apparent reason other than to confuse and befuddle out-of-towners, the fact that Bullfrog Road itself was wider and better maintained than the very driveway I had turned around in by the very slimmest of margins, and the fact that the green road sign had been knocked from its upright position to lean at a forty-five degree angle to the ground and had, in fact, been transformed by so much purple spray paint from the Bullfrog Road sign into an impressive, if not dangerously so, declaration of D.C.'s undying affection for L.J.

As soon as I parted ways with the highway, I began scanning both sides of the narrow gravel track for mailboxes, the plan being to count two such landmarks and turn into the drive accompanying the third. I expected this to be a relatively quick process. I was wrong. According to my trusty odometer, I had traveled over two miles of sludgy mud-rock aggregate before spotting my first. It was set up on two rusty tire rims welded together at right angles to one another and bore the surname of Settlemires. The second came about a mile later and was nameless. Remembering Rosie's rudimentary directions, I looked up through the swiping of my windshield wipers and saw what looked like an enormous green finger distinguish itself from the gray haze of the storm. Rising from the gloom on the left-hand side of the road was the silo she had mentioned, completely devoured by kudzu vines.

I turned in at the next opportunity and was faced with a cute brick cottage with wood-stained shutters and the most meticulously groomed flower beds imaginable. The grass was emerald green and had been trimmed recently and although it had been raining ceaselessly for almost twenty-four hours, there were no standing slush-puddles in the yard. I powered down the KIA in the driveway as close to the front door as possible and, with shoulders hunched against the wind-driven onslaught, scampered up to the doorbell and gave it a ring.

Immediately, the door jerked open and I was greeted in the portal by a scowling Miss Rosie. She spoke loudly over the din. "Oh, for heaven's sake come in, Mr. Johnston," she said as if I had been loitering about for hours. "If you insist on standing there on the stoop like a flipped-over stag beetle, you're liable to float away!"

three

Despite the rain and, of course, the incident that capped it off, it was an unusually pleasant visit.

She had me remove my shoes, which I did with a considerable amount of difficulty as I am in the habit of knotting and double-knotting everything, and place them back outside on the front platform. Then she took a moment to measure up my socked feet and, confirming to herself that there was no chance of my tracking anything through the plush coral-colored carpet that covered her living area, nodded in curt satisfaction. I was led to a stodgy arm-chair that was wrapped in a beige blanket as perfectly as if it had been professionally reupholstered and instructed to sit. As she shuffled off into a deeper portion of the house which I assumed to be the kitchen, I scanned about the room. There was no television, but rather at the place where one would expect such a focal point there sat a very antique-looking Singer sewing machine. It was still threaded and two large cuts of white fabric converged be-neath its needle. The rest of the room was a blur of framed black-and-whites photographs as Miss Rosie reentered from the rear of the house bearing a tray that, as I could see once she carefully set it down on the round sitting table at the elbow of my enshrouded chair, was crowded with porcelain coffee cups and saucers, a pot that steamed with the smell of fresh country coffee, a tiny bowl of sugar, one of creamer, and two pies, one of caramel and one of pecan.

I smiled gratefully and told her that I hadn't intended on her going out of her way to make a pecan pie simply because I had mentioned it as being my favorite. She swatted her bony hand in my direction. "Some things in life should always be your favorite," she said in that no nonsense tone that so many people mistook for harsh. "Pie is one of them."

And so we ate sweets and drank sweetened cups of coffee and although there was no television to provide those momentary distractions that glue together most modern day exchanges, the conversation never lagged and neither of us had to struggle anything out of the other or sit through an awkward lapse. We chewed and sipped as the rain droned on and on, beating her tin roof, not as the little fingers had played tap-tap on the Bakers' shingles, but as the large fists of angry men. However, somewhere between the inarguable perfection of the pies, for one would have to be a fool to dislike either, and the intrigue of eighty plus years of gossip, I barely noticed.

She started with folks I had met. Nora Jo, it seemed, had not always been so upright in her ways. Rosie had gotten it from Tommy Speth, the former Town Law, that Nora Jo had been caught parking up at the old pallet factory with Russell Forsight. All be it, that had been fifteen or more years ago when she was a poofy-haired sophomore at Millwood Branch High, but still it had happened. Furthermore, Miss Rosie was convinced that if that Forsight boy, as she called him, hadn't been brought up on burglary charges a short time after, our Preacher's Wife would have quickly found herself pregnant and all but outcast by the community instead of the First Lady of a congregation of the Lord's church.

As for Gene the preacher, she simply made a drinking motion with an empty hand, hiccuped as she lolled her head about drunkenly, and winked.

Then she moved on to people I didn't know. The principal down at the school was a dimwit with hardly the cognitive ability to dress himself. The town grocer had always leaned toward the prissy side but had only recently been seen in the company of another man with almost identical feminine characteristics. The current Lawman, Jim Motley, who came from a long line of lawmen-Motleys, had turned out to be quite lazy and spent more time holding down a chair and trading the news up at the Dairy Bar than anything else. And it went on and on until I had a rough picture of the entire town and I realized with no great surprise that Miss Rosie had respect for virtually none of them. And it was as this idea came to me that I discovered my saucer clean but for a few tiny crumbs and my cup empty but for a dark ring at the bottom and began to think of my shoes on the front porch and the unpleasant prospect of squeezing into my KIA wet to the bone.

I had just opened my mouth to announce my gratitude for the lovely desserts and the enjoyable conversation and yes, we should do this again sometime, when she set her own saucer back on the tray, leaned back in her rocking chair, and closed her eyes.

"Now Mr. Johnston," she said, her eyes closed and face quite tranquil, "tell me a story about flying. About the first time you flew. That'd be a good place to start."

Needless to say, I was a bit taken aback at this, but presently arranged my thoughts into a relatable enough story and again opened my mouth to speak. This time I was interrupted not by the peacefully patient old lady sitting across from me, but rather by the deafening boom and blinding flash of an extremely close bolt of lightning.

We were both startled out of our minds and for a moment Miss Rosie stared at me accusingly as if I had somehow called the lightning out of the sky. Then we ran to the back of the house into the room that I had correctly assumed as the kitchen and peered through the window over the sink that gave out onto the back yard. To the left of the yard, smoke was rising from the blackened remains of a split tree trunk. Luckily, everything was too wet for there to be any real concern for fire. The rest of the oak, which a mere thirty seconds before had been quite alive and quite strong, was laying in the yard like a massive piece of broccoli. We both stared at it for a moment in which the correct polite consoling words eluded me until finally Miss Rosie looked up at me with one artificial eyebrow cocked and said, "Mr. Johnston, I do hope you know how to run a chainsaw."

I remember tittering nervously and making a quip about not being much of a man if I didn't, having no idea that she was in fact quite serious until I got home that evening and checked my answering machine. There were two messages from the airline concerning upcoming flights and one very recent recording of a familiar elderly woman's voice. Familiar, yes, but gummy as if her dentures were soaking in a cup on the edge of the bathroom sink. She never identified herself on the message and I guess that would have been deemed gratuitous information for someone such as Rosie Cotcher. Instead, she gave a very detailed description of where the saw was located in the shed out back and a warning that it would require fresh oil and gasoline as it had been some years since it was last cranked.

four

It took me the better portion of two months to finish with the fallen oak which Miss Rosie said had been planted by a Settlemires at the conclusion of the Civil War shortly after the entire region was burned by an offshoot of Sherman's strong right arm.

There were a number of reasons the job consumed such a chunk of my first summer in Mississippi, with Mother Nature laying claim to some and my gracious red-headed host to the others. Firstly, the heat cannot be overstated, though the toupeed meteorologists on the local networks gave it a worthy try, and yet the words one could put down in an attempt to describe such temperatures and the exhausting oppression they invoked would be typical and the real-time experience was anything but. Suffice it to say that July and August were hot and the air was congealed with moisture and those conditions alone would have hampered and deterred even a hardier man than myself. Secondly, the tree, as I mentioned, was as old as the South's Restoration and had a myriad of branches that had to be sawed off and hauled away as brush before the trunk, which was more than two feet through the center, could be considered. Thirdly, and the last with ties to any natural cause, was the condition of the chainsaw. Not only was it in need of oil and gas, but the chain and blade had rusted together, the toggle that controlled the choke had either been knocked off or chewed off by some long-gone vermin, the air filter was gummed with an unworkable amount of oily sawdust, and all the lines were dry and cracked and in need of replacement.

Miss Rosie, embodying the consummate supervisor, provided her own distinct set of distractions. Before the actual sawing began, she seemed to be a never-ending source of "why don't you"s and "what if you"s, each carefully toned to implicate my utter ignorance of the task at hand. It quickly came to the point that her constant and subtle suggestions passed directly through my ears without discussion or debate, the only evidence of such being my unconscious leaning toward her directions. I took comfort in the prospect of the loudness of the saw's two-stroke operation and the blaze of the now shadeless backyard, thinking quite naively that the combination of the two would force Miss Rosie indoors. Instead, she threw on a sun-visor that seemed to me to be made of corduroy and pointed her knuckly finger here and there, signing me through the work the best she could.

And I was only able to work on Thursdays. I had taken on a number of additional flights to repay time lost over the last turbulent year and that squeezed down on my days off, leaving me with only Thursday on most weeks. Furthermore, I was having a difficult adjustment to the extra two hours added onto my round trip commute to and from the airport. So between the challenging exterior conditions and the tightness of the invisible leash Miss Rosie had fastened around my neck, not to mention to the limited supply of Thursdays in a given week, the first two of which were spent restoring the primordial chainsaw to a usable state, I need not be ashamed of the two months it took me to vanquish the great oak.

But, you might ask yourself and rightfully so, why? Why would I submit myself to such unpleasantness when I was under no legal or ethical obligation and never promised or even hinted at any financial reimbursement whatsoever? The answer is both complex and embarrassingly simple. I was new in town and felt that excluding myself from any activity with any of the indige-

nous population would all but put a lock on my status as an out-
sider. In addition, in spite of the heat or maybe even because of it,
I began to view the job of dealing with Miss Rosie's oak as a necessary rite of passage, as if by completing the job I would earn the
authority to live in the country amongst country folk. Overarch-
ing all of this was what most people would likely define as
chivalry but I, being far more familiar with myself and my general
lack of romanticism, saw as the impracticality of a very old
woman with a very large tree down in her backyard, no matter
her oddly-ribbed visor and capacity to withstand the elements.
For all of that, the simplistic neanderthal side of me was capti-
vated by the frequent glass of the best homemade lemonade and
the cellophaned platters of cookies that were prepared for me to
take home once I called it quits for the day.

five

But before I get too carried away, let me tell you about Old Man Settlemires and that first Thursday I had the chainsaw in full operating condition. That was the day of our initial introduction. Although, as I look back on it, we never were *actually* introduced, per se.

Miss Rosie and I were in her backyard. I had been staring at that enormous oak for some time, drawing a diagram in my head, erasing it, starting over. After several attempts, I settled on what I considered to be a suitable means of attack and was just about to yank the crank-cord on the newly-refurbished saw when we heard the crunch of gravel and the deep warble of a diesel-fueled engine. As I bent and laid the saw down in the grass, I could feel the sun's blaze burning straight through my shirt and, not for the first time, internally questioned my ability to work in these temperatures.

"Tell me what you see 'round there," Miss Rosie said jerking her head toward the road.

I raised up and craned my neck to peer around the corner of the house. There was a large brown pick-up truck, the kind with an extra set of wheels on the rear axle, coming to a halt in Miss Rosie's driveway.

I told her it appeared she had a visitor.

"Is it a big ole step-side truck?" she asked. "Kinda poop-colored with a vomity-yellow strip down the fenders?"

I wanted to laugh at the accuracy of her description but she didn't seem to be joking so I just said yes ma'am and bit my tongue. And it was a good thing, too, because when she turned on me there was no mistaking her seriousness.

"You let me do the talking, you hear," she said. "Sebastian Settlemires can be a mighty fair-skinned devil if you ain't familiar with him, but he *is* a devil, so you better just let me handle him. Just keep on looking at that tree like you've been doing."

Just then I heard the truck door slam shut and before long, an old man was hobbling down the hill toward us. He wore a pair of overalls high and tight, just under the armpits, over a long-sleeved flannel button-up despite the heat and the heat index, the sun and the humidity. Although he was making good progress down Miss Rosie's back slope, he walked with a cherry-wood cane in one hand, swinging it out in front of him and leaning on it with each step. When he got close, he tossed the cane up and caught it near its midpoint. Then he used its gold handle to point at the downed oak. Although the sun thrown back from that gold was almost too bright to look at, I found myself unable to look away.

"See you got yourself a tree down, Rose."

Miss Rosie didn't look at the tree. She didn't look at the gleam coming off Settlemires's cane handle, either. What she did do, was fold her arms across her chest and look dead into Old Man Settlemires's sun-browned face.

"It ain't Rose, it's Rosie," she said. "And to you it ain't even that. To you, it's Miss Cotcher. Ain't that what you called me in those court papers? *Miss Cotcher*?"

Settlemires put his cane back on the ground and leaned against it. He shot me a quick glance and let loose a forced chuckle before continuing.

"Now there's no need on not being neighborly, is there?"

"Neighbors don't take each other to law, *Mister* Settlemires."

"Now I've put that in the past, Ro-," she shot him an acidic glare and he stopped short, "okay...Miss Cotcher, and I'd hope you could do the same. That was those pulpwooder's lawyers' doings, like I told you, and I put an end to it once I found out, didn't I? And apologized profusely, might I add. But like I said, that's over and done with and it most definitely *ain't* why I'm here today."

It was an odd feeling, standing there listening to this conversation. I felt as if I were an eavesdropper, as if I had snuck up and was listening from behind the barn instead of out there in plain view.

"Well why *are* you here?" Miss Rosie asked. "Here. On my land."

Again, he slid his eyes in my direction. I could tell he had questions about me he wanted answered but that the opportunity for those questions hadn't yet presented itself. He pointed with his cane again.

"Just heard you had a tree down in that gully-warsher we had awhile back," he said.

Miss Rosie unfolded her arms and held them out toward the leafy branches of the oak. "Well, you heard it right," she said. "There it lays, but not for long. We're cutting her up just soon as you get on."

Settlemires stuck a thumb behind one of his overall straps and regarded the tree with a long purposeful scan, from where we stood, all the way up its length and then slowly back. He blew air through his pursed lips and shook his head, making sure to spare me and Miss Rosie's chainsaw laying at my feet a calculating look.

"Tree's probably planted by one of my great-great grand-uncles. Pip Settlemires probably, right after the war." He swung his cane in a wide circle. "My Paw used to say ole Pip planted all these old oaks 'round these parts. Them Settlemireses planted pine and blackjack and sweet gum, too, but Paw always said Pip was partial to oak."

"Your Paw used to say a lot of stuff, didn't he," Miss Rosie said.

They looked at one another for a moment and I could tell there was something in that statement to which Settlemires wanted to respond. He appeared on the edge of saying it too, his lips opened for it, then he just shook his head and went back to looking at the tree.

"Sure is a big one, ain't it?"

"It is."

He looked at me, gauged me up, and there was no mistaking it this time.

"Reckon it's too big for just one saw?"

"We can manage it, thank you," said Miss Rosie.

"I gotta crew, mostly Mexicans, can chop that tree up and have it outta here by tomorrow if you'd let me."

"You know I don't want none of your bunch up here cutting anything."

"I won't put a charge on it."

"We can manage, thank you." She said it sharper this time.

At that, Sebastian Settlemires nodded and appeared willing to push the issue no further.

"Good day, then," he told the ground at Miss Rosie's feet, apparently unwilling to meet her eyes. He nodded to me as if to imply that I was included in his well-wishes. Then he turned and made his way back up the hill. I wouldn't exactly describe the manner in which he left as whipped and I wouldn't exactly say his tail was tucked between his legs, but I can tell you this much; he sure didn't go up that grassy slope as spry and lively as he had come down.

As soon as he had ambled out of earshot, Miss Rosie turned to me and pointed at the chainsaw.

"Have you got that thing figured out?"

I said I had.

"Then crank it up would you Mr. Johnston, and cut something with it before he drives off," she ordered. "And make it look like you know what you're doing even if you ain't got a clue."

So I did.

six

Fast-forward now. Past the rest of the tree-cutting, past the heat.

It was the last Thursday in August and I was just the other side of Settlemires's mailbox when the realization hit me that there was no more work to be done. The previous week I had piled the usable stove-lengths, amounting to over two full cords by my amateur estimation, in Miss Rosie's front yard as she had made arrangements for a Mr. Dillinger from Littleton to come that Saturday and haul the lot of it away. If he was to pay for it, I never asked and wasn't told, being contented with the fact that it was over and done. And as if to punctuate the entire ordeal, the saw, new chain and all, had been placed back on the corner shelf of the shed for the sweet Southern air to destroy once more.

That had been a week ago and yet there I was cruising down Bullfrog Road with as much speed as the loose gravel would allow and coming to as if snapped out of a deep hypnosis. I shook my head and made another of my signature quips, this time to no other audience but myself, about the peculiarity of muscle memory. Giggling freely at my own expense, I decided to turn around in the silo-house's driveway and was just about to flip on my blinker, again by virtue of sheer muscle memory because the only vehicles I had ever seen on this stretch of Bullfrog Road were Miss Rosie's two-ton Chrysler, my own KIA, and the occasional burdened-down pulpwood truck pointed in the direction of Highway

354, when I noticed the cookie platter bouncing along on the passenger seat beside me. I removed my hand from the turn signal. Since my silly little trance had brought me that far, I figured it might as well take me another few hundred yards and allow me to return the platter and chalk up this trek not to my own premature senior moment, but rather to a good deed well done.

As I pulled alongside the little cottage, I was struck with the beauty of the day. It was late August, as I have mentioned, and the intense ultra-white blare of the summer sun had given way to a golden textured ambience of Autumn-to-come. The unsightly piles of split firewood were entirely gone from the place, as Mr. Dillinger was satisfactorily greedy in not leaving so much as a scrap of bark behind. The flower beds on either side of the front walk had been recently tended. The mulch was fresh and chocolate dark with bundles of red and orange mums dotting the front of the house with color. It was all very Norman Rockwell, and the rooster weathervane spinning lazy on the roof was the cherry on top.

If I hadn't known better, I would have said I felt a pang of regret that there was nothing more for me to do other than return the borrowed platter and drive back to the Baker House. But certainly I *had* known better and it was just as I was assuring myself that it must be a pang of a different origin that I came to a stop in Miss Rosie's driveway. The instant I killed the engine, I heard the slam of the front screen door and the *swish-swish* sound of Miss Rosie's slippered feet on the walk. As I rose out of the KIA, I found myself quickly wrapped around the shoulders in an old bed-sheet that smelled strongly of scented fabric softener. My confusion must have been written all over my face.

"What?" Miss Rosie asked defensively. "You'd rather have hair down your shirt?"

I remained at a loss, but grasped onto the two concrete nouns and sputtered them back at her as one word interrogatives.

"Yes," she intoned as if helping along a child with special needs, "a shirt is what you've been wearing on the upper half of your body since you came out of onesies and hair is this stringy stuff growing out of the top on your head. See, when the stringy stuff gets too long, as yours has done," and she gave a handful of the finer hairs on my neck a tug that truly hurt, "you cut it off."

She was right, I realized. My hair, usually well maintained and cut in the fashion that I jokingly referred to as The Cary Grant, had begun to cover over my ears and broom the white collars of my pilot shirts. Still, I had used the same East-Memphis barber for the previous four-plus years and was, and still am if the truth be told, overly particular at best and down-right ornery at worst about the how and by whom my hair is cut. And so, I protested. Or tried. She only allowed one singular word of it.

"But nothing, Mr. Johnston," she said as she pointed around the house to the carport where I could see the butt-end of her Chrysler backed halfway out onto the drive. "Go on around there and have a seat while I go back inside and fetch a bucket to collect the trimmings." And then another stab of the finger and, "Go on now, get. If you piddle and I have to finish up by moonlight, you're likely to draw stares tomorrow and I don't mean the good kind. Now," a third and final finger stab, this time with an added twist as if to drive the point further home, "get."

And so, after momentarily entertaining the thought of dashing to my car, spinning out on her gravel driveway, and roaring away down Bullfrog Road, I did as ordered and I got. The front screen door smacked shut behind me as the satisfied Miss Rosie went about her fetching. Feeling quite like a wrongly chastised child, I stomped past the Chrysler, the sheet still draped about my shoulders, and plopped into a rickety Windsor chair that had been placed in the area vacated by the front end of the lengthy automobile.

After a minute or two of silent fuming, Miss Rosie emerged from the back door carrying not one but two old gallon ice cream buckets, one of which was empty and presumably for gathering what she had called the trimmings and another that was filled with grooming utensils of all sorts. There were multiple scissors; why there were more than one pair remains beyond me. There were electrical shears and a plethora of different sized guards all thrown into a hodgepodge. Combs, brushes, tweezers, razors, and even one or two metallic gizmos for which I do not have a name. She dropped this bucket onto the table at the back of the carport and to my mind, I heard it clank and rattle with all the torturing charm of a dungeon master's bag o' goodies.

Then without warning, her two knobby hands grabbed my head on either side and pushed my chin down to my chest. I felt the fine teeth of a comb scrape down my scalp from the crowns to the nape of my neck and I must have jumped. "Now, be sure to hold still," she said. "If you wiggle, you might lose an ear." Then came the first few snip-snips and I froze solid, moving only when her hands pushed or pulled or jerked or spun my head into a new position.

"There's something I'd like to speak with you about, Mr. Johnston," she said after a few quiet moments in which the only sounds were the snipping of her scissors and the whisper of clipped hair falling lightly onto the blanket about my shoulders like snow. "Something I've hoped you might help me with." I was still very uncomfortable and leery to move even a fraction of an inch, but she seemed to wait on some response from me before going on, so I blurted some indiscernible thing out through my clenched teeth, silently and fervently praying that it wouldn't cost me the pain of losing an earlobe.

She continued. "I'm dying. But that's no great unexpected thing. At my age, you're either already dead or you're dying from something. Just the way it is. It's how it's happening that I wanted to talk to you about. They found a tumor, right up here." I ventured a peek up at her as she was standing to my side and saw her tap a finger on her temple. "Right up there in the old noodle." Then she grabbed my head, one hand on the back curve of my skull and one under my chin, and with no great gentleness pointed it forward once more. "Now you hold still or we'll end up shaving the whole thing off like Mr. Telly Savalas."

But being still is a difficult task when the woman cutting your hair lets slip that she has a brain tumor, that the doctors don't know exactly when she'll lose her marbles, and that they were giving her pills so she doesn't lose all of them at the same time. She came around to my front and began combing my hair down my forehead. Suddenly I was extremely aware of the sharpened points of the scissors and their close proximity to my eyes. As the scissors snipped their way across my forehead, I held my breath and pinched my eyes shut with enough force to explode purple and red blossoms on the interior of my eyelids like Chinese fireworks. Finally, it was over and I realized she was talking.

"Smile, Mr. Johnston," she was saying, her fists planted impatiently on her hips. "Don't you know what 'smile' means?" I looked back at her as if her marbles were already missing. Why would I smile when you just told me you were dying of brain cancer that look said.

"Or if you know of a better way to raise your ears, do that. But smiling's the best way I know." So I smiled at her and I felt the hair tickle the tops of my ears as they rose. But it was nowhere near a genuine smile as the gravity of Miss Rosie's situation began to settle on me. She squinted down one eye and worked her tongue subconsciously around her mouth as she slipped the scissors over my left ear and gave a snip that sounded more like a chomp. Then she squinted the other eye and did the other side, that silly superficial grin still on my face. Then she parted my hair with a couple of deft swipes of her comb and took a step back.

"Now," she said with a nod.

After another moment of appreciating her own handiwork, Miss Rosie stepped over to the table and dropped the scissors and comb back into the bucket. There was a loud clinking and clanking as she began rummaging around for another tool.

"I *am* dying, Mr. Johnston," she said as she searched. "But I'd rather that the entire town not know about it. I get tippy-toed around and stared at sideways enough for just being old and I don't want more such foolishness for fear of me going bananas and running around town in my night gown, heaven forbid." Then the noise ceased and as she turned towards me, it was evident that what she was about to ask stung her pride. "To be clear, I'm not asking you to babysit a dying woman, that would be too much. But I wondered if you wouldn't mind popping in every week or so, as you've been doing, and maybe even picking up my pills. The druggist down at Baxter's is as crooked as a dog's hind leg and if he ever got 'hold of my prescription, by nightfall half of Hickahala County would know I's dying and the other half would think I's already in the ground."

She took a deep breath and seemed to steady herself. Then she held something out to me and my hand had to fight its way free of the blanket to take it. It was a mirror, small and round and scratched. I held it up and looked at myself. It was amazing; Miss Rosie had given me the best haircut I'd ever remember having. If the conversation had been lighter, I probably would have winked at myself and said "Ju-dy, Ju-dy, Ju-dy". Instead, I looked into my reflected eyes and asked Miss Rosie if anyone, anyone at all other than her doctors, knew of her condition. From the corner of my eye she shook her head. And why, I asked, did she trust me? I pointed out that she barely knew me, knew nothing, in fact, of my life prior to two months ago. And she chose to entrust this secret with me?

"Did you know I've lived here in this tiny town my entire life, Mr. Johnston? My entire life." Her eyes glossed over and began to wander. "I remember the day they paved our first road. I remember when the men of the town would meet in the school auditorium to organize that year's crop. I remember when the fire department auctioned off their horses and bought their first engine. I remember a whole slew of firsts, Mr. Johnston, and I've known a whole slew of folks. Every grandmother, mother and daughter, every grandfather, father, and son that's passed through this town. I know where they've been, when they got there, who they went with, and what they did while they were there. Sometimes I could wish to know less."

She took a moment and then her eyes refocused and she fixed me with a stare. "I know you won't rob me," she continued, "or you'd already done so. I know you're a church-going man and I know that airlines aren't in the habit of hiring maniacs to fly their planes. Other than that, you're right, I don't know you from Adam's house-cat. And I believe, Mr. Johnston, that is why I like you."

seven

Time flew. For the next three or so months, my entire existence was a ball-bearing rolling in a long straight groove. Minutes passed as seconds, days as minutes, and months as days.

The only reliable measure of time was the changing of the seasons and the shortening of the days. By November, although it was still warm enough for short-sleeves on most days, everything had changed from green to brown. The trees which dominated the rural skyline were naked but for the flocks of black-birds that fluttered and squawked from one to next. Leaves stood in mountainous drifts on the windward sides of fences, houses, and barns. The Wilbanks twins, which were the town's only hired hands and the co-proprietors of a single brain, had begun to decorate the downtown area for Christmas, a week-long undertaking that a single more capable man could have completed by lunch the first day. I stood in my front yard and listened as they argued for twenty minutes over whose turn it was to ride the lift and hang the wreath on the streetlight nearest my house.

As for Miss Rosie, nothing appeared to change. She remained as sharp-witted and razor-tongued as ever. At her behest, I began to sit with her on the first pew each Sunday. Through the singing, she would lean over and whisper in my ear about so-and-so three rows back or so-and-so wearing the white blouse on the back pew and after a month of Sundays, I knew everything there was to know about the members and frequent visitors of our small congregation. If Gene's sermon wasn't to her liking, she would snort and shuffle in her afghan and shake her head, disguising her displeasure not an inch. If the sermon was agreeable, the church's temperature would be unbearable. Either hotter than the blue blazes or cold enough to hang meat, she'd say. Each Sunday she would threaten Gene with a move of her membership and tithe if these faults did not meet with a speedy correction. I developed a sympathetic respect for the preacher and thought that between his wife, whose presence I had come to loath, and the incessant bickering of Rosie Cotcher, being a prisoner of but one vice was a feat to be admired.

Shortly after Labor Day, I repaid the last of my flight debts and for the first time since my relocation, my schedule began to open up allowing me the opportunity to complete the task of transforming the Baker house into my home. I painted both the kitchen and the extra bedroom as the bedroom had been a neutral khaki and the kitchen had been papered with a floral print that resonated the seventies, both as a decade of origination and the approximate age of the house's owner and chief decorator. By Thanksgiving, all the cardboard boxes were emptied, all the furniture was arranged, and all the pictures were hung. I even took the liberty of stenciling my last name onto the mailbox.

As was the arrangement, I kept Miss Rosie's condition in confidence. Yielding to her mistrust of Baxter's, I used a pharmacy in Memphis on the Millwood Branch side of the airport to fill her prescriptions, popping in with such frequency that the check-out girl would grab the bag of medicine marked Cotcher when she saw my KIA pull into the parking lot. Then I would pay Miss Rosie a visit every Thursday, delivering the medication and settling up the charges, for which she refused to trust my word and insisted upon inspecting the receipt before handing over the appropriate amount of money, always in cash and always in exact change. Then we would sit and eat sweets and drink coffee. She never thanked me and surprisingly, this never bothered me. I was in that groove and for those three months, nothing seemed to bother me. For the first time in a long time, everything felt situated and in the proper place; the past behind and the future ahead.

And then came the week after Thanksgiving.

eight

For those in the commercial airline business, Thanksgiving is not a holiday. In fact, it is quite the opposite. If you can sort luggage, book flights, push a cart down the center aisle and hand out complimentary packs of nuts, and certainly if you can fly, Thanksgiving week and the weekend which follows are primetime. You work, fly your plane or push your cart or sort your bags or whatever. You sleep when you can and where you can. The rest is a blurry haze that you use your love of flying to justify.

The following Monday, the last in November, I awoke in my bed at the Baker House and immediately shuffled into the kitchen. I needed coffee. It wasn't jet lag I was suffering from, it was shear mental exhaustion, but I was suffering none-the-less. And a nice cup of coffee was just what the doctor ordered. I could sit on the front steps as the sun climbed over Main Street, setting the auburn treetops on fire, and sip on my coffee and zone out.

I squinted against the bars of sunlight slicing sideways through the kitchen and, in my fragile-yet-reckless early morning condition, stubbed my pinky toe on the cabinet baseboard, darn near tearing it clean off the side of my foot. Although I have never, even at my rock-bottom lowest point mind you, been prone to foul language, I cussed and did so loudly, with conviction. Stumbling forward, I pushed past the canister I had characteristically, and appropriately, labeled **sweetener** and popped the top on the adjacent one marked **coffee**. Inside, there was nothing but the shiny bottom of the canister and a tiny wooden spoon.

Then I cussed again.

Fifteen minutes later, my KIA swung into the parking lot in front of Shop-Rite and out popped a slightly limping, fresh coffee jonesing, jogging pants wearing me. The hope of my zonking out on my front steps and digesting what remained of the sunrise was still harbored somewhere inside my brain, but the realization of that image required coffee.

Coffee. Aisle seven at Shop-Rite. Wedged between the syrups and cereal bars. Quick in and quicker out. That coffee would be abrewin' in less than ten minutes. So fixated on the task at hand was I that the poop-colored dually parked half-in-and-half-out of the front handicapped slot never registered.

I leaned against the door and pushed off my good foot and came face to face with James Sebastian Settlemires, that fair-faced devil but a devil none-the-less. He was dressed exactly as during our first meeting, bib overalls pulled high, flannel shirt buttoned under his chin and down to his wrists, but this time he was wearing a hat. It was a typical give-away hat, high foam front panel and mesh everywhere else, a braided rope strung across the top of the bill. In big yellow lettering the front read **Bluetick for Supervisor** and was garnished with a matching yellow outline of a hound with one front paw raised in a point. I was just discerning between the possibilities that the hat was a joke, like a gag gift from some country store that doesn't mind exploiting the terms redneck and hillbilly for profit, or that Bluetick was the surname or nick name (more likely) of an actual person when Settlemires spoke.

"Morning young fellar," he said, hooking the golden handle of his walking cane over the baby blue handlebar of a shopping buggy. "Johnson is it?"

I corrected him, placing emphasis on the T but omitting the obligatory comment as to the commonality of the mistake. To my own ears I sounded rude and blunt and *closed*, as if the sign hanging on my storefront read Gone Fishin' and my lights were out and my door locked. But all that didn't seem to deter Settlemires. He swung his buggy around and made for the produce stands at the left of the building and, unexplainably, I followed step in step.

"I see," he said. "John*ston*. Not plain-ole Johnson like Lyndon B., that ole bastard, but John*ston* like, well, like Albert Sidney." He wheeled his buggy to the side of a large pallet of dog food, which if you ask me has no place anywhere near the produce section, and shouldered a bag from the top of the stack and dropped it into his buggy. Then he propped his elbows on the blue handlebar and continued on to the bananas.

"They say," he continued, "that Albert Sidney Johnston was the finest officer in the whole Civil War, North or South, before he was killed up at Shiloh. Say he had a way of motivating his men that ain't been seen before or since. Better than Old Stonewall, better maybe than General Lee hisself. Took a bullet behind his knee and bled out, Albert Sidney did. I seen the place they say he died, up at Shiloh, under this great big tree. They got a monument there now, you can read all about it. Hell of a thing to see."

Settlemires parked his cart and pulled a plastic baggy from the roll, fumbled it open with his arthritic fingers. He pushed his cap back on his head. Then he scanned over the three-tiered banana display with his eyes. He picked up a bunch, held it roughly three inches from his face, inspected it, mumbled "too green", and set it back. The next was "too ripe", although from my vantage it appeared the identical shade of banana-yellow as the first, as them all in fact. As this process drug on for four or five rejections, I became convinced that my presence was a forgotten thing, a trifle, pale in relation to the comparison of produce adequacy. Just as I was about to slink off in the direction of aisle seven, Settlemires dropped a five-banana bunch into his plastic baggy, which he laid in the child seat of his shopping cart with meticulous care, pulled the bill of his cap back down to its accustomed position, and resumed our conversation, that is to say *his* conversation as I had contributed but one word, as if it had never paused.

"Hell, come to think of it, I knew a Johnston once myself. In Korea. Paul was his name, or Peter or John. Philip maybe, I'm not sure. It was a Bible name though, if memory serves. Anywho, us boys just called him Piss Ant. Had a sergeant called him Private Piss Ant straight through drills, from the very first day we got off the bus to the day before they shipped us out it was Private Piss Ant this and Private Piss Ant that. Earned that nickname honest, too, wetting his britches if you just looked at him funny. Not the military genius Albert Sidney was, was this Johnston, although they ended out about the same. Reckon he's any relation of yours?"

I wasn't sure if he meant the ill-fated general from The War Between the States or the ill-fated private with an overactive bladder from the Korean Conflict, but as far as my response was concerned, it didn't matter. I told him that to my knowledge, no, there was no relation. He was inspecting cantaloupes and gave no indication that he heard me.

"You did good work on that oak up at Rose's. Took you near the whole summer, but my Paw used to say 'nothing good gets done in a hurry' and I reckon I hold to that." Then he held a cantaloupe against his ear like a seashell and thumped it with his thumb. To me it sounded like a thumped mellon, to him, I can only imagine. "Hope you weren't put off by our little run in. I's just trying to offer a kindness - tree-cuttin's my business if you ain't been told - but Rose, God-bless-her, she ain't never gonna see nothing I do or say or think as kindness. On account of our history."

Settlemires shook the cantaloupe the way a child might shake a Christmas present. Then he put it to his ear and thumped it again. He shook it some more, listened. I made the mistake of asking what had happened between them, him and Miss Rosie, to strain their relationship so. The old man shushed me and pressed the mellon tighter against his ear, his brows furrowed in concentration. After what seemed like hours, he grunted and put the cantaloupe back, leaned on his buggy and pushed on.

"'No shame in honesty'. My Paw said that."

He took a few more shuffling steps and then stopped. Suddenly, I became acutely aware of the fact that there were no other shoppers in our vicinity. There were no sounds beyond the soft twang of Merle Haggard through the overheads, no bouncing head-tops to be seen on the next aisle over. The entire store, as it would seem, was ours.

"I want that land," he said, looking down past the buggy's handle at the black-and-white chessboard tile. "Her land - and it *is* her land, I ain't never said different - ain't much. Forty-five acres all told, minus a couple for the houseplace, a few more that's swampy and good for nothing but snakes and 'skeeters. But even forty good acres is a big deal when you're in the business of contracting out to pulpwooders, as I am. I'd pay an honest price for it of course, offered to more times than I can count, but Rose won't have it. She don't have a use for it, ain't got a young-un to pass it down to, nothing, and she wouldn't sell it to me for all the tea in China."

I asked why he thought that was and he turned his head and cast me a sideways look. For a moment, his face bore an odd expression of contemplation, as if he were searching for the answer himself. Then he looked down the aisle, narrowed his eyes, and got his buggy rolling again. I got the sense that my time of following him through the store had come to an end so I stayed put.

"If I knew, I'd tell you," he said walking away. "But I don't, so I can't."

I watched until he rounded the corner at the back of the store and disappeared. Then, an idea hit me, an image equal to that of myself sitting cross-ankled on my front steps. But with the added bonus of my curiosity on the Settlemires Situation, as I had begun to think of it, being satisfied.

I left Shop-Rite empty handed and drove the KIA out to Bull-frog Road.

nine

Miss Rosie kept trying to feed me, but all I wanted was the coffee, and the conversation.

"First thing's first, this plot of land is *mine*. It was my daddy's before he died and it's passed to me fair and legal as can be. Second thing - are you sure you wouldn't eat some French toast or buttermilk biscuits or anything, Mr. Johnston?"

Again, I assured her no. Coffee, just coffee, was fine.

"Okay then, suit yourself. Now where was I?"

I told her she was at the second thing.

"Right; the second thing. The second thing is...well I can't remember what the second thing was exactly, but the first thing is that this is my land and that can serve as the second thing and every other thing too as far as J. Sebastian Settlemires is concerned. I can't help that his Paw held on to the soybean business for two harvests too long. I can't help that his Paw ran outta money at a time that money was scarce. Or that his Paw sold this plot of dirt to my daddy for a song. And I *definitely* can't help that his looney-tuney Paw signed it over to him on the back of an empty carton of cigarettes."

I nearly sputtered on my coffee and burnt the back of my throat in the process.

"Oh yeah, you didn't know? Paw Settlemires - the 'Old Man Settlemires' when I was young - took a little bit of squirreled-away cash and a handshake from my daddy and my daddy took these forty-five acres and a signed carton of Viceroys as a deed of sale. Their mail carrier, a man by the name of Turner, witnessed it and signed the carton too. Things like that happened all the time back in those days."

I asked if I could see the cigarette carton and when she faltered, I asked if she still had it, already knowing what her answer would be.

"Daddy always kept that carton in the rolltop desk there in the living room. He'd take it out every once in a while when he thought I wasn't looking and gloat over it like a pirate gloating over a pile of gold coins. When I's little, right after he bought this place and we built the house, he'd take that carton out and wave it over his head and whoop and pat his hand on his open mouth and do this Indjun warrior dance 'round the room. He knew that always got me tickled. But he'd always tuck it back in that rolltop, middle shelf on the righthand side."

I asked her if it was there now, in the middle righthand shelf of the rolltop, again already knowing the answer.

"After my daddy died, I never laid eyes on that cigarette carton. I didn't have a reason to. Until I had a visit from the constable, come to tell me Settlemires and his lawyers had drawn up and filed papers contesting my ownership of daddy's land. Said if I wouldn't mind showing him proof, papers and such, then he'd get on back to Littleton, file a report with the circuit judge and that'd be that. Well, I ain't never been so embarrassed in my entire life. I went straight to that rolltop and wouldn't-you-know-it, that Viceroy carton wasn't there. I looked through all the shelves, all the drawers, I dumped it all out there in the middle of the living room, and it was nowhere to be found. I told the constable to hang on and I went back to the bedroom and went through my closet, my shoe boxes, my sock drawer, everything." She shook her head. "Nothing."

I asked what happened next, my coffee mug all but forgotten.

"Constable left, said he'd see how it played out but if he were me, he'd be expecting a court summons in the mail. So I did. Walked out to the box every morning expecting to see a brown envelope stamped with the courthouse's return address. For two weeks this went on. I was as jumpy as a cat with kittens. Then one morning, I walked out there and instead of a letter, there was Sebastian's pick-up truck and Sebastian hisself."

She took a sip of her own coffee and I thought about asking her what Settlemires had said, but then everything snapped into focus and I didn't need to. Settlemires had dropped the suit. He didn't need to see the lost carton of Viceroys to validate Miss Rosie's claim to those forty-five acres. He'd probably seen it before, maybe even on the day it was signed, only he was too young to be an official witness so fortunate Mr. Cotcher and desperate Mr. Settlemires asked the mailman to be so kind as to lend his signature. But even if that was overindulged speculation and he'd never actually seen it, he'd heard about it. He'd heard his Paw grumble on and on about those forty-five acres he'd signed over on an old pack of his favorite brand of smokes.

"Funny thing is, me and Sebastian used to be good friends. The kind of neighbors that'd look out for one another, you know the kind. But when something like that passes between two people, it changes things. You start to see the bad in 'em. You see the excuses behind the apologies. The motives behind the offers. They say time heals all wounds but I reckon that only works with a certain type of person. For other folks, like me and Sebastian for instance, time festers all wounds." She sipped her coffee again and made a scrunched up face. "My coffee's gone cold, Mr. Johnston. I'm going inside and zapping it in the microwave. I could whip up some scrambled eggs and toast, too while I'm at it."

As if on cue my stomach growled. My curiosity had at last given way to my appetite for sustenance. I relented and let her fix me breakfast. And we never discussed the Settlemires Situation again.

ten

I remember dialing the numbers. My mouth had gone suddenly dry and no matter how much I swabbed my tongue around, it just kept getting drier. My finger was numb and shaking as it punched out the last few digits. This was foolish, I thought, and on impulse, I nearly slammed down the receiver. The only thing that kept it to my ear was the knowledge that hanging up like a skittish teenager was even more foolish.

It rang. And it rang.

Finally, a click, a rustle, a voice.

"Hullo?"

My own voice sounded distant and immature, small. "Tiffany?"

"Yes?" She sounded confused. There was music in the background. Bing Crosby crooning a Christmas tune. And other people talking and laughing. "May I ask who this is?"

"Tiff, it's me." She knew who it was, she had to. You can't forget someone that quickly no matter how much they deserve it. "I just wanted to call."

Long pause. Bing held on to every single note with pregnant purpose.

"Eric, have you been drinking?"

"No, no, no. I just wanted to call. It's the holidays, Tiff and I just..." Now I paused. There was not a drop of moisture in my mouth. All the moving parts had stuck together. Visions of Miss

Rosie's lemonade filled my mind. Just the right mix of tart and sweet and hydration. My kingdom, I thought, my kingdom for a drop of lemonade. My throat was clicking and the words croaked out. "I just wanted to call."

"Okay." She was impatient. I had interrupted something, a party maybe, and it was in her voice. "Well, do you need anything? Is everything okay? Are you? Okay?"

Bless her. At that moment, I felt a collection of emotions that is difficult to describe; shame, pride, sorrow, disgust, love. Yes, there was love still in me. I blinked through tears I hadn't known were there.

"I'm in a good place, Tiff. A real good place, I think. I have a house. It's not the newest house, or the nicest even, but it's clean and quiet and I like it. Maybe a little over-organized, but you know me." I tried to laugh but it didn't work. My breath caught like a piece of wool on sandpaper. "I'm going to church every Sunday now. It's a small church way back in the sticks, but they're nice folks and have taken me in."

"That's great, Eric. That's really...great."

"How was Thanksgiving? Did you visit the Freemans this year?"

A pause. "Eric, I really don't have time..."

"Is Megan there with you? I'd sure love to talk to her. I bet she's getting to be a little chatterbox."

She took a long deep breath. "No, she's not. I mean, she *is* a chatterbox, talks all the time. But no, she's not here with me. Look, Eric. Right now's not a great time."

In the background, White Christmas had changed to Blue. Mr. Presley never sounded so sad and alone.

"Of course. I understand. Of course." And then quickly, "I've got an extra room. A small bedroom. Worked really hard getting it all fixed up. There's a daybed and a little plastic kitchenette and glow-in-the-dark stars on the ceiling. It's all fixed up. I worked really hard to get it done by Christmas."

I think she was crying now, but it was hard to tell with all the background jabber. Her voice shook. "It's not a good time. I have to go now."

A click and it all was gone; her muffled sobs, the party-like chatter, the Crooner and the King. There was the bone-hollow dialtone, and after it droned on for what felt like years, an automated voice instructed me to hang up the phone and try again. The first part, I obeyed.

eleven

    Winter arrived and right on cue.

    It took three attempts to crank the KIA and on the third and ultimately successful endeavor, the ignition sounded reluctant at best. It was cold and the air was damp with a swirly mist that might as well have been snow and my car, it seemed, preferred not to leave its garage. But at my insistence, it finally tumbled over. The tiny four cylinder engine rattled to life and I was on my way.

    Main Street was, as much as it pains me to compliment the handiwork of the bumbling brothers Wilbanks, elegant and festive with just the correct measure of Christmas cheer. As I turned from my driveway onto Main, I paused for a moment to appreciate the view. The streetlight wreaths were all up and hung out over the street at perfectly matching heights and angles, shrinking smaller and smaller off into the distance. I could see the brightness of Baxter's large storefront window which was bordered with holly and garland. Inside, one could see a beautiful lighted tree and a toy train chugging in a slow circle around it. All the businesses up Main Street were similarly decorated; the hardware/Co-op, the law offices, and even the infrequently-visited shoe store. All of them. And then as if presiding over the entire street, the Town Tree stood at the southeast corner of Main and Highway 354. From my vantage, even a cynic would have found the view beautiful and it was no surprise that as I made my way down the middle of this Christmas cornucopia, my lips reflexively puckered and a medley of whistled carols mixed with the thump and knock of my warming engine.

It had been weeks since I had last used Miss Rosie's doorbell and when I got to her house and didn't see her sitting in her usual place on the front porch bench, my mind immediately took to worrying. Even with the weather, I expected for her to be waiting outside wrapped in a cocoon of thick blankets. But the bench was empty, so I shoved the gearshift up to park, jogged to the front door, and gave the bell four or five quick anxious rings. Nothing; all was quiet. I made a fist and rapped the metal framework of the screen door loudly. Silence. I began to shout her name and banged a couple more times.

In the stillness that followed, I strained my ears. I'd forgotten to switch off my engine in my haste and it was difficult to hear with its idling directly behind me, but I thought there was a faint voice calling. I shouted her name again and this time I was sure there was a distant reply. In an instant, my mind had formed a horrific image. She was hurt and needed help; I had to get inside. I swung the flimsy screen door aside and tried the doorknob. It was locked and sturdily so. Her voice drifted out to me again and whether by an increase of effort on her part or my own imagination, it seemed louder and more distinct. Panic hit me and on its heels came the notion of smashing through one of Miss Rosie's windows. I bounded into the yard and, plucking up one of the bricks that bordered her flower bed, took direct aim at her front window.

"Stop, you!"

I hesitated, brick raised over my head like a Sandy Koufax baseball card, and turned toward the side of the house. There was Miss Rosie in her cocoon, just as I had envisioned, with nothing uncovered except for her head and an angry pointed finger. Her face was a scowl and that finger was pointed at me.

"That brick was made from the same red clay you're standing on and is older'n me," she said as she advanced on me, her massive bundle of blankets swishing. "The window-glass would probably shatter it rather than the other way 'round but I'd like to not find out, if you please." I was still frozen mid-pitch, the brick cocked at shoulder height and my mouth wide open and gaping out frosty breaths. She hopped up and with her only exposed hand, snatched the age-old brick from me. As she bent and with extraordinary care set it back in line with the others, I rediscovered my voice and feebly attempted to explain my actions.

She hardly listened.

"It'll never go back just like I had it," she was muttering to herself. "Never, oh never. Ah well, there's nothing for it. Just have to rig it for now and redo the whole thing come April."

Finally, she straightened and examined the line of bricks. It was impeccable; a perfect line of red-maroon bricks, the top edges of which slanted with precisely the same lean. Even I couldn't tell which one I had nearly flung into Miss Rosie's living room. "Just have to redo the whole thing in April," she repeated with a surrendering shake of her head. Then she turned and looked up at me as if I had just arrived.

"Merry Christmas, Mr. Johnston," she said showing her dentures. "You have work to do before dessert so you might as well get started."

twelve

She led me around the corner of the house and we were nearly to the gambrel-roofed shed when I snapped my fingers and jogged back to kill my engine, which I had completely forgotten in my haste to break into a house and rescue a dying woman. As I jogged back down the hill toward the shed, a light flickered weakly for an instant and then shone out constant as Miss Rosie wired a high-wattage shop light to an old car battery. Then she hung the light on a small chain that dangled down from a rafter, casting the shed in a bizarre series of naked unrefined whiteness and deep shadows.

"Christmas stuff," she said pointing up into the rafters. "Boxes and boxes of it. And it all needs to go inside. Ladder's in the corner," and she pointed, "but do take care. It's got a trick step or two. I'll be inside sorting through what you bring." Then her hand disappeared into the blankets with the rest of her and she waddled out of the shed, calling back over her shoulder. "And making the spiced tea, of course."

I watched as she reached the back door and vanished inside the warmth of the house. It was most likely my imagination, but I could have sworn there was a hint of cinnamon on the cool air as the door swung shut behind her. Cinnamon or not, imagined or not, there was definitely something more than the stale dirt-smell of unused yard tools, so I stood there for a moment and breathed it in. Then I shook my head and set to work.

The ladder Miss Rosie had referred to was an all-wooden fossil that weighed nearly a hundred pounds. I was unable to tote it all the way to the center of the shed in one effort, stopping every two or three steps to search for a better grip and catch my breath. Once I got it to the appropriate place and unfolded, I rested for several minutes, panting and flexing out knots in my forearms and biceps.

Contrary to her warning, every step was a trick step. Climbing the ladder was an exercise of intense concentration, balance, and luck. Each rung pivoted with varying degrees of ease so that if one's ankle was not set and locked before one's weight was transferred to the foot belonging to said ankle, one would be flung to the ground. As I climbed the ladder for the first time, two thoughts flittered through my mind: one of a black-and-white Three Stooges' ladder gag and one of flannel-clad Canadian lumberjacks logrolling.

The loft of the shed was decked with thick sheets of plywood that sagged in the spaces between the support of the rafters. I panned my head left and right, mindful not to shift my weight as the step beneath my feet felt overly liberal. To the right, was a large uneven sheeted mound. Dust and dirt lay heavy on the sheet and pooled in its low places. Whatever was under it hadn't been seen or moved since well before last Christmas. To the left, however, was a fresher stack of boxes, each bearing layers upon layers of faded masking tape at the various points of entry. Moving with extreme caution, I lifted the closest of these boxes and placed it on my shoulder. It gave a reassuring jingle. Then I started a descent, which was nothing more than a controlled fall.

For the next hour I worked, climbing and balancing and carrying. I never gained the confidence to bring down more than one box per climb, no matter how light or manageable that box might have been. Then I'd walk up the hill and shift my load to one side or the other freeing a hand. Warmth radiated out to me like the impending embrace of an old friend at the first crack of the door.

Miss Rosie used a dull steak knife to slice open the boxes and as soon as she lifted the flaps and saw something red or green or glittery, she'd shoo me out into the cold for another. It must've taken me twenty trips, but finally the left-hand side of the loft was bare except for a peppering of mouse pellets, a few capsized cockroaches, and one last lonely cube of taped cardboard.

There are a number of famous quotables on the subject of curiosity and not all of them paint the intellectually inquisitive in such a negative and devious light. And while these thoughts and musings, mostly on the part of renowned men and women of science and mathematics, are no doubt true, they bear very little weight on my specific case. No, one need look no further than the most famous and, in fact, basest of these observations to describe my motives and resulting actions on that last trip up the ladder into Miss Rosie's loft.

I peered to the left and saw, with a considerable amount of relief, the last box. Then, I looked right and suddenly knew that I had to know what lay beneath that filthy sheet. It was nosey, of course, and wrong but the morality of it all was a far-off train that had yet to come to station. I placed my palms on the plywood and hoisted myself up onto the right-hand side, the cold of the wood wasting no time soaking through my pants and freezing my buttocks. Then, I swung my feet over and troll-walked the three steps over to the oddly-shaped mound with the boards sponging beneath my weight and my knuckles nearly dragging. There was no room to stand, so I dropped to both knees and with a flurry of sediment of all varieties, whipped the sheet away.

On the very top was a framed photograph of a young woman. It was Rosie Cotcher; smiling, smooth-faced, early-twenties Rosie Cotcher. Even in black-and-white she was attractive. She wore a uniform of sorts, dark padded jacket and matching bobby-pinned cap, and there on the lapel, gleaming in the light of a flashbulb, was a set of pinned wings. I gaped at the photo and thought back to our first introduction, how Miss Rosie had changed when Nora

Jo mentioned my profession. Delicately, I set the frame aside and dug deeper. There was a cracked leather-bound chest and the hinges whined like a pinched baby as the lid fell back. Inside were more photos, grainier and less-professional than the first. Young Rosie in front of a small prop-plane, a smile as big as the sky. Another of her in a pants-suit, leather cap, and goggles. She was removing a pair of gloves and regarding the photographer with a playful smiling-frown. Rosie at an old grass field air-strip, one hand flattened above her eyes to shield away the sun. A plane blurred by in the distance.

Up the hill, I heard the backdoor creak open.

"Mr. Johnston!"

I put the photos back into the chest and slammed the lid, momentarily unable to answer.

"Mr. Johnston, is that it? I still can't find my Santa Claus punch bowl." There was a hesitation, then, "Mr. Johnston? You-who?"

That was when curiosity, as the saying goes, quite nearly killed the cat.

I scrambled back to the ladder on all fours and as my left foot touched the top rung, time slowed to an unreal pace in which I could see what was about to occur before it happened, but lacked the ability to alter the natural course of things. It was as if I were watching a bad movie for the second time. My foot on the top rung. My weight shifting from the stability of the loft to the rickety dishonest ladder. The step pulling a trick, the cruelest of them all. My ankle giving way. The whiteness of my hands groping like claws for something, anything. The cold air rushing around me, my breath a fog above me. The roof. My scream.

The dark.

thirteen

There were voices, some I recognized and some I'd never heard. They drifted in and out like a turn-dial radio searching for a station. Behind it all was a garbled beep and a slow steady *suck-hiss, suck-hiss* like mechanical breathing.

"...check of his status?"

"Same as before, limited to zero response to..."

Fuzz and static as the dial spun. Drifting, drifting. Rise and fall on the waves of consciousness. Rise...and fall...

"...walk? Let's not get ahead of ourselves here..."

Long bray of static and then nothing. Nothing for ages.

"...been asking to see him."

"You mean like, visitors?"

"...very insistent, even threatened to go to the Board of Directors..."

The beep grew louder, more concrete, like a real thing in a real world. I paddled my little boat in search of its shore. Paddled with cupped hands that felt weighted with lead.

"...ladder's been in my family for years, decades, and never once..."

"...better today. B.P. is up and stable. Tactile stimulation is still..."

Easier and closer but the weight was still there. That crushing weight. The suffocating pressure reserved for nightmares.

"..can't talk to you, honey, but the doctor said he might could hear..."

"Mommy? Mommy, dat don't look like Daddy..."

"...come around soon. Maybe this week he'll be..."

Everything felt heavy. The weight of the world was on my body from head to toe. Like I had sunk into quicksand. Opening my eyes was an epic struggle and the lids fluttered before they raised enough for me to see. The world was a great white blinding blur. I blinked. That hissing and beeping continued over my right shoulder. On reflex, I tried to turn towards it but quickly found I could not. Gradually my vision cleared and I could make out a grid of ceiling tiles and fluorescent lights. Then a familiar face rose into view like...like a red rose sprouting from the soil.

"Now don't you try to talk or move or anything," Miss Rosie said in a hoarse half whisper. "It'd do you no good. You're in the I.C.U. at Methodist and for a bunch of non-immersers they're pretty good folks. Good doctors. Said you might try and fight a bit when you came to, but I'm telling you there's no sense in it. Just stay put and we'll get the whole story from the doctors when you liven up some more, 'K?" She nodded. "Okay."

My mouth worked but all that came out was a series of erratic smacks and the same *suck-hiss* of artificial wind. She must have read my lips.

"Yes, yes, they were here. She's a very pretty young lady, your little Megan. Very nice to talk to. Quite the princess. Now, rest. There'll be time for everything else when you wake up. Rest, rest..."

My eyelids were fluttering shut even before she finished. The sterile whiteness dimmed to the black again and I was soothed into a dreamless sleep by the gentle lullaby of the ventilator that for the past seventeen days, had kept me alive.

fourteen

As you may surmise, the following six months were the most trying of my life. I was a newborn, in effect. Fragile, incapacitated, and grossly dependent. Most days I didn't care to live. I am unabashed to say in no uncertain terms, that if I'd had the means to commit suicide, I would not have hesitated to do so. Initially and for quite some time, there was no survivor drive. No inner will to overcome. And as I scan back over those first difficult months, only snatches of time are available to my memory as if the majority of those weeks and days and hours are too dark and dire for my psyche to re-endure.

I remember my first conversation with a doctor. I say *a* doctor because there were so many during my stint at Methodist Hospital and each more forgettable than the last. It was their similarities, not their subtle disparities, that complicated their individualism. Each had dark to graying hair, well-maintained and parted to the right. Some had glasses and some didn't, but the glasses were the rich type with glare-free lenses and hardly a frame to speak of, designed to inspire the doubt of their existence in both the wearer and the viewer. And they all wore long white coats over pressed shirts and ties, cufflinks flickering back reflected light when they adjusted their feather-light spectacles or ran a raking hand through their salt-and-pepper hair. It was like naming each and every variation of a Mr. Potato Head and, in my uninspired condition, I gave it an equally uninspired effort and gave up with haste.

The first Dr. Spud Jug's name was Granville. That I do remember, and most likely because Granville was his first name, not his last. I couldn't help but wonder about the sanity/eccentricity scale and how poor baby Granville's parents measured up at the time of his christening. It is an odd thing to remember to be sure, but I like it. I take it as evidence that somewhere beneath all those wires and tubes and bolts and screws, the same quirky, quippy me was still alive.

Most of what Doc Granville told me that day, with an elevator version of piped in Jingle Bells providing melody to the monotonous *beep-beep-suck-hiss* in the background, I had already figured out. I had fallen. A vertebra in my neck had been broken. Shattered, rather. I was quote **lucky to be alive** end-quote. My spinal cord was miraculously undamaged in the fall, which is why I hadn't died instantly. They had to perform surgery to piece back together my neck-bone, of course. C6 was comprised more of metal and alloy than anything else now. The halo around my head and the four screws affixing it to my skull were to keep the damaged area immobile. To allow the bone to heal. Amazing piece of technology, he said, genius. And then his face turned down like a child 'fessing up to peeling back the corners of Mommy's new wallpaper. The procedure had caused some inflammation. In what he so coldly referred to as The Cord. And some inflammation in The Cord is enough to cause paralysis. And that is where I was. Paralyzed from the neck down. Was it permanent? And this was his last word. Doc Granville stated my fate in one noncommittal breath.

"Maybe."

I remember the faces of my visitors. Empathetic and hopeless faces. Nora Jo and Gene came. Nora Jo talked and talked but I didn't hear a word. Gene held a hand I couldn't feel and asked the Almighty for healing but above all else, His will be done. Pilot friends came and went, each whispering condolences and avoiding my eyes at all costs as if my seemingly disembodied head was Medusa's. I was at my own funeral, in my coffin and watching the processional line. Before long, the faces all blended together and the only things of which I was vaguely aware were that, in the days and weeks since I had paddled clumsily out of the murky waters of my coma, Rosie Cotcher had hardly left my room and Tiffany and Megan Johnston had yet to come.

fifteen

Tiffany O'Meary was born to sturdy strong-willed Irish parents on the banks of Elliott Bay in Seattle, Washington. She often joked that her folks had settled as far from their native land as possible without leaving the continental United States, citing that the frequent rain had reminded them of home. And that was usually all she would allow on the subject in general conversation because in the summer of 1979 when Tiff was no more than three years in this world, George O'Meary and his rosy cheeked wife, Lisa, took a weekend drive through Oregon and never came back. George, it had seemed, had fallen asleep at the wheel and wrapped their '75 Bel Air around an electrical pole, which were at that time as scarce in the state of Oregon as the Irish were in Washington.

Three-year-old Tiffany's babysitters had become her first foster parents.

Throughout her young life, Tiffany O'Meary was shuffled from home to home, zig-zagging her way back and forth across the country. As far as I could tell, she was never harmed or mistreated by any of her caretakers, but the nomadish lifestyle itself left its mark. She grew up quickly. And when we met years later on the campus of the University of Florida, her issues concerning trust and abandonment were already well-ingrained.

I was a young man with the keys to the world in my front pocket having just received my certification from a nearby aviation school. Some friends and I frequently cruised through Florida's campus looking for pick-ups and when I spotted Tiff leaving the student union with the setting summer sun in her pale blue eyes, I nudged Paul Glassier, who was driving at the time, in the ribs and told him to *pull-over-pull-over-man-there-she-is*. Her parents might have left her early in life, but that old Irish strength was in the blood and if anything, had grown stronger by fending for herself for the previous twenty years. That first meeting ended with her slapping me sharply in the face and telling me to go suck an egg someplace.

But I was persistent and the next day, she didn't slap me. She did cut her eyes, those beautiful eyes, and scowl and stalk off without a word, but I wasn't slapped and that kept me coming back. She was a tough nut to crack, that young Tiffany O'Meary, but as I said, I had the keys to the world and eventually I won her over. We fell in love. And as hard as she resisted in the beginning, she fell all the harder. Her love, I soon learned, was an all-encompassing thing, complete in reach, large in stature, and without condition - save one. Every relationship worth its salt is founded on the principle of exclusivity, but ours laid its cornerstone there. Although it was never stated in words or written in a contract, there was never any doubt: If I ever wandered, if I ever cheated, there would be no second chance.

We got married. I moved our two person family to Memphis for a job with Gulf Coastal. And for a few years, we settled in. Everything was grand. Tiff had had a mega-rich foster mom in Des Moines that had set her up with a modest trust fund and we used a chunk of it to purchase a house in the East Memphis hills, which I happily organized from basement to attic. I flew a light schedule of flights around the Mid and Deep South. Tiff started a book club with some ladies in the neighborhood and I went out with my pals from the airline every two or three weeks. It was a good life and looking back on those early-Memphis years, I realize that perhaps they were too good, too settled, too *standardized*, at least for Tiff. She began to get antsy. She sipped her coffee anxiously in the morning as if waiting for bad news. Her questions about my fidelity, which were always a part of our vocabulary, increased to a daily confirmation that I had not taken a lover. She became more physically clingy and more emotionally distant, if such a thing is possible. Her mood escalated each and every day to the point of crescendo. And then one Autumn morning as I was brisking out the door with a buttered bagel clenched between my teeth and my overnight flight duffle in my hand, Tiffany O'Meary Johnston told me she was pregnant. *We* were pregnant. And as those pale blue eyes studied me for a reaction, I dropped first the bag then the bagel and finally myself as the shock left me lightheaded and wobbly-kneed.

Eight months later, I found myself the father of a very precious unplanned baby girl and the husband of a woman I wasn't sure I knew. I couldn't shake the thought that Tiff had gone off the pill to trap me in a marriage I hadn't wanted out of. I loved Megan from the moment I saw her, don't get me wrong, but more and more, Tiffany's paranoia was rubbing off on me and I felt, *could actually feel* myself becoming the man she feared I already was. Soon after Megan was born, I stopped attending church. That was the first domino. Then came the drinking. And more drinking. I never flew under the influence. That sacred trust at least remained a holy ground that I, even at my rock-bottom lowest point would not consecrate, but I'd be lying if I said I didn't go through many-a-preflight with cottonmouth and fidgety near-shaking hands. And we stumbled on like that for months, more for the baby than for ourselves. Deep down, I think we both knew it was over.

Finally I cheated, in a full-tilt drunken stupor for which I am and will always remain thoroughly embarrassed. The details of that muggy Miami night I will omit out of respect for the other parties involved. As for myself, I deserve none. I have come to loath the hazy memories I am cursed to carry from that night, but even then the shame was immediately suffocating. It was as if a plastic bag had been duct taped around my heart. I broke down and told Tiff the very next night after the baby had been tucked away in her cherrywood crib. Once I could bear the act of meeting her striking blue gaze, I saw the look on her face was as much of vindication as hurt or hatred. I expected her to slap me across the cheek the same way she did on the day we first met and when she didn't, it hurt. The other shoe had dropped and if anything, I believe she was relieved that the waiting was over.

She threw me out that very night and except for two custody hearings, one preliminary and one gavel-to-gavel sorrow, I had not seen Tiffany O'Meary since.

sixteen

His name was Jeremy. He wore dark navy scrubs and a pony-tail.

"Mr. Johnston, are you ready to learn to walk?"

I would have nodded but my head was bolted to what the good Doctor Granville had referred to as "an amazing piece of technology" but for all I could tell, looked like a piece of metal from a scrap heap.

"I mean, are *you freaking ready to walk, baby*? And you better be sure too, be *real* sure. Because this ain't gonna be no lolly-gag. I can personally guarantee this is gonna be the hardest, most frus-trating piece of work you've ever been up against. And you're gonna cry, you believe that? You might not even be the crying type, I don't know. Might not have cried when your momma and daddy whipped your baby-butt, might not've cried at Old Yeller even, but for this you will. But you wanna know something else? I can guarantee you something else, too, Mr. Johnston. You give me all you got, you lay it all out there, and I'll have you up and walking. *You will walk.* It's a guarantee."

Then he spun around and with one hand, pulled his ponytail to the side. A long white scar dripped down the center of his neck. He spun back around. A feverish grin lit his face.

"I have been there, down that well. I know that hopeless-ness."

His face got closer and closer to mine until our noses nearly touched.

"You will walk."

Then he gave the tiniest of nods as if to provide punctuation to the whole affair. His eyes blazed one last flare of excitement and he left. My room had a television mounted in the corner, but it was dark and silent. Everything seemed still and quiet in Jeremy's wake like the calm on the backside of a tornado. All I could hear was the drip of my IV and the soft *click-clack* of Rosie Cotcher's needlework.

seventeen

Slowly, slowly I got better.

I began breathing on my own. The first few gasps felt like blunt stabs in my throat and a million-billion tiny crackles in my chest. The doctors declared it a good sign that I could feel anything at all below the neck. To me, it felt like pain. But as each breath grew easier, as the crackles shrank to a thousand, a hundred, a handful, I began to come around to their optimism. For the first time in months I was able to control my own *suck-hiss* sounds.

My trach-hole healed. I began eating real food again. Miss Rosie took one dubious look at the first tray of hospital food and immediately turned up her nose as if they were serving cowpies. The next day she brought a brown paper sack filled with tupperware. She hand-fed me pork tenderloin, sweet potatoes, black eyed peas, and cheddar biscuits and when the hospital lunch arrived, little Miss Rosie shooed the orderly away, brandishing a plastic spork like a switchblade.

My sleep-wake cycle began to resemble that of an average human and that, if nothing else, seemed to boost my mood out of the ditches of utter despair. I would keep the blinds open through the day and watch the clouds. The sky is an unfathomably wonderful piece of artistry and some days I would watch it until my eyes burned.

"I know that look."

I was snapped away from the window. This was late March and my C6 had healed as well as it ever would. The halo was gone, perhaps thrown back into the landfill with Doctor Granville's other genius devices of immobilization. My mind had wandered, lost somewhere out in the big blue, and I hadn't even noticed that Rosie Cotcher had bundled up the sweater she was working on in her lap and was watching me with curious eyes. My neck was stiff to be sure, but I rolled my head to face her.

"Look?" I asked, still a bit scratchy. "What look?"

"The look like you know something real good but you're just now seeing it for the first time. It's love, that look. I may be just an old maid, Mr. Johnston, but even I know that."

I turned back and looked at the sky. The edges of my eyes stung.

"But it's not just looking you're doing," she continued. "It's thinking, too. Thinking about will you ever walk again. But mostly about will you ever fly again. You miss it something fierce don't you?"

I blinked away the stinging wetness in my eyes. I didn't want to talk about it. Everything Miss Rosie had said was the gospel truth. I was thinking those things. I did miss flying, that freedom in all degrees that is impossible to achieve on land, but I didn't want to talk about it. It was like describing a mouth-watering feast to a starving man. Even so, I shouldn't have gotten angry. But I did.

"Do you, Miss Rosie?" I shot at her. "Do you miss it ever? I saw your flying things, you know. In the shed's attic. I saw the pictures. I know you were a pilot and I also know you're not one now, so *you* tell *me*. Do *you* miss flying, Miss Rosie?"

She looked back at me. Her face was steady and calm. She didn't lash out, she didn't point her finger, she didn't do any of the normal Miss Rosie things. And my heart, buried in a chest that I could hardly feel, instantly broke open. Finally, she turned her head and took up my view, looking out the window and seeing what I can only imagine.

"My great granddad and his brother were yankees, can you believe it? They grew up New Jersey or New Hampshire or someplace like that. Rufus and Carl Cotcher had been their names. When they got to be teenagers they decided to hop on a train and head out on their own. Well, you wouldn't know this, but the ole tracks there in Millwood Branch were at one time linked into a great big system of passenger lines. Not anymore, of course. Amtrak changed all that and now all we have is the City of New Orleans line coming up and down through Memphis. But back then, loads of folks came through on those tracks. Anyhow, Rufus, that was my grandaddy's daddy, got off the train there at Millwood Branch and, on a whim, decided to stay put. Carl just kept right on riding; if memory serves, he ended up out in Texas someplace. Well, besides being yankee, Rufus Cotcher was an airplane man. 'Course, it was all very new back in those days and flying wasn't something that all that many folks could do. The way my grandaddy told it, Rufus worked hard for a number of years doing odd jobs here and there and mising away every nickel and dime that didn't put bread in his belly until finally he had enough to buy himself a strip of land. And that was the R. and C. Cotcher Airstrip. First one in the area. Named it after himself and the brother he hadn't seen in years. And it was a booming whop of a success. All the crop-dusters flew out of R. and C. and in a place like Millwood Branch, Mississippi, there was and still is more than a small number of fields that require dusting. When Rufus died, my grandaddy took it over and when he passed on the count of a bad case of the asthma, my daddy did." She was still peering out into the sky. Her voice was steady, but I think she began to tear up. "My daddy didn't have a boy, he only had me, and the crop-dusting business had about dried up by then anyway, so he sold the airstrip land before I hit twenty-five. But I grew up in an airplane, Mr. Johnston. Learned to fly before I learned to drive an automobile or break a horse. I grew up with the air over me and around me and under me. I grew up out there, in that blue. So, yes. I miss it."

That told the largest portion of the story, but it didn't tell the entire thing. There was a gap to be filled in and I thought this might be my only shot. She had already opened herself and I just wanted to reach in and get one more little thing.

"But they don't give silver wings to crop-dusters," I said.

She looked down in her lap and fidgeted with the near-complete knit sweater, twirling yarn around a knuckly finger.

"No, they don't. They sure don't." And I thought she might just leave it at that, might slam the doors shut. But after a moment she looked back up at the sky and bridged the gap. "There was flying to be done in the War, quite a lot of it, and not all was combat flying. They sent the boys to do the worst of it, of course, but they still needed qualified pilots, even women pilots, to fly things and people back and forth across the country. By then, daddy's mind was set on selling off the airstrip and it was my only chance to get into the air. So I volunteered. And that's how I got my silver wings."

"Miss Rosie?"

She didn't even turn her head towards me. "Yes?"

"You have that look now."

She turned. And then she smiled. Suddenly she was that young girl again, the one in the black-and-whites under the sheet in the shed's loft. She wasn't an old woman dying of brain cancer. She was a twenty year old red-head with a set of silver wings and a flat hand on her brow to shade out the sun as she watched the planes. And I realized that what I needed, we both needed. We were passengers on the same bus. We didn't get on at the same stop and our destinations might have been leagues apart, but for a time, we were riding along together.

"Miss Rosie," I said; I, with the ability to turn my head but not to lift it, to twitch my fingers but not to grip, not to squeeze. "I promise you this: we will fly again."

She smiled at me again and nodded. Then we both turned back to the window and watched the sky.

eighteen

Jeremy had been right. I was crying.

They had wheeled me into the physical therapy area which was a long baby blue room on the first floor. We were surrounded by racks of free weights. Resistance bands dangled from wall pegs like moistened spaghetti. There were grab bars and pulleys and cushioned platforms, some set at a normal height and some clearly meant for wheelers like me. The room looked and felt like a gymnasium for the special olympics. For me, it was no more than a show, a head game. I wouldn't be able to do any more down here than I would up in my room and Jeremy knew it. But he thought it would inspire me. Instead, it felt like being paralyzed in a deep ravine and looking up.

"First rule," Jeremy started as he always did, "is never, *never* take a step back. So, let's do what we know we can do."

I looked up at him and took a deep breath. Even though I knew he had once been in my position, even though I knew that alone should demand my respect, I think I hated Jeremy. He stood there on his two good legs and I hated him. But a corner of my mind also knew that by hating him, I was playing right into his hand. Jeremy wanted and needed for me to hate him. And, at that moment, I did.

"Come on," he said. "Do it."

I looked down at my hands. They were balled loosely in my lap, nestled on the soft fabric of my hospital clothes like two dead doves. I put a thought in my head and focused on making it happen, making it real. Nothing happened. Those hands weren't mine. Somebody else's. The puppet strings were cut.

"I said do it."

My anger flared like a stoked fire. My concentration doubled. Again I pushed the thought down the pipe between my brain and those two dead hands that had landed in my lap. When nothing happened I pushed it again. And again. I don't know how long I pushed. Somewhere along the way, Jeremy had gotten into a crouch and was barking out encouragement or threats that I barely heard. I didn't need to hear to know what he was saying.

Taking a step back. I was taking a step back.

Suddenly, I became aware of something small and distant. At first, I interpreted the sensation as a pinprick, but almost immediately realized that wasn't quite right. Something on my hand glistened, just below the big knuckle of my index finger. I looked at it curiously. Dimly I became aware that Jeremy had shut up. As I watched, another tear fell from my face onto my hand.

And I felt it.

I was crying, just as Jeremy had predicted. I didn't know I was, I hadn't realized in my epic struggle to move my hands, but I was crying all the same. And as the salty water struck my hands, I could feel it. I shifted my focus onto the sensation. I gathered up everything I had and pushed back. The old channelways opened up. There was a twitch. And weakly, my hands came back to life. I flipped them over with a sobbing grunt and began to touch thumb to pinky, thumb to ring finger, and so on.

Jeremy stood back up.

"Okay," he said nodding. "Okay."

But he only allowed me a moment's complacency.

"Now, raise your arms."

I looked up at him, tears drying on my face, a face that surely reflected my inner incredulity. We played a quick game of mental chicken and for a moment, neither blinked. I thought about asking him if he was serious, if he had perhaps lost his mind somewhere between thirty seconds ago and now, but that honest corner of my mind knew he was serious and sane. That part of me wanted to raise my arms, wanted to walk, wanted to run the Boston Marathon and just keep on running. But at that moment, the rest of me was tired of the effort and even more exhausted with the prospect of a nearly certain failure.

At last, Miss Rosie broke our silent struggle of wills. She had been sitting on a padded bench which ran the length of light blue wall, but now she was standing beside Jeremy. She reached up and patted his shoulder. Jeremy blinked, coming down from his height of intensity.

"Why don't you take a breather for a minute?" she asked him and pointed over to the bench. "Let me see what I can do?"

She was sporting a pink jumpsuit that only women over a certain age could possibly wear. She was old and small and appeared as fragile as expensive China. Her dentures were perpetually flecked with red as if she had chewed her lipstick. But Jeremy found nothing comical about Miss Rosie. He hadn't known her long, but already he knew that Rosie Cotcher did not come as appearances advertised. Jeremy let his head sink. His shoulders relaxed. Then he slumped away towards the bench, but before he got too far, he called back over his shoulder, "But we *are* raising our arms today. This is *not* a give-up."

Miss Rosie turned back to me. I was still going through my exercises; thumb to pinky, thumb to ring finger, thumb to middle finger, thumb to pointer, and back down the line. It is an impossibly difficult concept to articulate, bringing your body back to life piece by piece. My hands were moving, by some inexplainable combination of intense focus and ingrained muscle memory they were moving, but they felt very far away. They were separated from me by the great gulf of my arms. They were miles away.

Jeremy still had his back turned, his ponytail just long enough to hide the scar on his neck. Miss Rosie waved a dismissive hand in his direction. "Forget him for a minute," she said. "He's too close to the problem." Then she centered me in her sights. "But he's right. You are gonna raise your arms today. Now, I've gone through a lot of trouble to make sure this happens so you just don't let me down, Mr. Johnston. Sit tight. I'll be just a minute."

Then she waddled off down the length of the room, her pink pants swishing out a repetitive whisper. I looked questioningly over at Jeremy, who had just gotten settled on the bench along the far wall. He appeared as clueless as I felt. When she reached the door that let out onto the hallway, she swung it open and gestured for someone to follow her in. A womanly shape filled the threshold. A woman carrying a bundle on her hip. A bundle with a head full of golden ringlets.

So many things happened at that moment. I saw Tiffany O'Meary, not Tiffany O'Meary Johnston. I saw the young woman that had slapped me in the light of the Florida sunset. I saw the woman I had pledged to love, to honor. I smiled weakly at her and felt the sting of fresh tears. Miraculously, she smiled back.

And I saw the daughter we had made together. It was like seeing her for the very first time. I was in another hospital not thirty minutes away, the maternity ward at the Metro. I was wearing a pilot's shirt and slacks under my scrub gown having rushed straightway from the airport. The doctor was seated between the stirrups. One of my hands was gripping one of Tiff's, my other held her arm above the elbow. A nurse sat opposite me and did the same. The doc said push and we all pushed. We breathed and we pushed again. He said this is it, now push, push, push. We did. There was a deep collective breath and we knew she was out. There was a sound, a lovely little sound between a cry and coo. I looked at Tiff and smiled, weakly. And miraculously, she smiled back. Then the doctor was holding her out to me. So delicate, so delicate. And I raised my arms to receive her.

I was shaking. I was weak as water and shaking like a leaf on a tree in a windstorm but I was holding her in my arms and I knew I needed to be strong. I swept a lock of her ringlets from her forehead and she smiled up at me and stole the very heart from my chest.

"I been missing you, Daddy."

I looked up over my little girl's head. Tiffany was standing along the far wall with Jeremy and Rosie Cotcher. I blinked away the blur and mouthed the words, "Thank you, thank you." I meant them for all three of them, but especially for Tiff. Then I looked back down at my little angel and told her that I had missed her, too. I had missed her this much. And I spread my arms as wide as they would stretch.

nineteen

There was the day that I became acquainted with Mr. Leonard Buford Gay, Attorney at Law.

I was in my bed and Bob Barker was on the television. Miss Rosie absolutely adored Bob Barker. When those curtains parted at ten o'clock every weekday morning and he came sauntering out onto center stage she always pointed and said, "Now there's a man with class." She chuckled at all his jokes and doted at his every wink. The act of missing a single show was a trespass she considered with near equality to sin. In fact, her morning ritual of watching The Price is Right had so imprinted itself on me that I naturally flipped the channel over to CBS every night before falling asleep in anticipation of the following morning. I even watched when she wasn't there, which was the case on that particular day.

The contestants were placing bids on a fine set of European-styled flatware and that's not all, a fine washer/dryer combo made by Maytag, Maytag the leader in supplying your every appliance need. Thank you Rod and thank you Barker Beauties, what with your revealing hand motions above and around the mahogany case of forks and knives and spoons and especially for wheeling in that massive set piece with the washer and dryer on cue. And why were those set pieces always carpeted with what looked like astroturf? The contestants had their backs to the stage, trying to interpret their friends' suggestions, struggling over the decision to bid for one dollar or one dollar more. I was mumbling out my own suggestions, another guilty habit I had picked up from Miss Rosie, when I heard a brief but unmistakable knock on my door.

Wondering who it was since the breakfast cart guy (along with the lunch cart guy and supper cart guy) had been sufficiently warned from my room by the repeated antics of one Rosie Cotcher, I invited the knocker in. And immediately in he came, Leonard Buford Gay on his top-dollar business cards and to his Mammie when he's in it deep with her like the time he was twelve and dropped a full carton of eggs and got caught putting it back in the fridge, Lenny B. Gay Lenny B. *Real Real* Gay to the mean chanting soulless kids on the playground back at Messick Middle School, L.B.G. to his more affluent and politically minded friends, and Scum of the Earth to me. As he slid smiling into the only home I'd known since my upside-down swan dive from the top step of Miss Rosie's trick ladder, my thoughts lit upon Count Dracula and the unenviable fates of those naive enough to invite him into their dwelling places.

"Mr. Johnston, hello," he said as he offered his hand.

I welcomed him nicely enough but did not shake his hand. I could have; by that time Jeremy had me up to fifteen pound dumbbell lateral raises, and twenty pound curls (Jeremy didn't flatly ignore any area but his true zeal was for working what he called "show muscles"). So it wasn't my physical inability that left Mr. Gay with an unshaken hand that he eventually and casually returned to his side, it was just a bad vibe.

"My name's Leonard Gay, Mr Johnston. I'm just here visiting a cousin up the hall and thought I'd stop by."

I thought about asking him if he always had a cousin in Methodist Hospital. Or an aunt, or a brother-in-law, or a somebody. Then I thought about maybe asking him for his cousin's name, demanding for it, and laughing as he struggled to come up with one. Of course there was no cousin, it just sounded better than saying, "My sleaze-ball contact inside the hospital was screening for potential cases and, what'd'ya'know, you're name just popped right out, so here I am to press the flesh."

"Terrible thing, that cousin of mine. He's in a situation a lot like yours actually. Hurt. Recovering. Been in the hospital for months." He was shaking his head in sympathy or disgust but that lawyerly smile was still there. "And did you know he has never once considered the cost? Oh, I'm sure he's thought about the physical toll his injury has taken on his body, but I'm talking about the *cost*. *Money*, Mr. Johnston."

I told him that I had a job, that I had insurance.

"Oh sure," he said, "your insurance will help, but unfortunately, it will only do so much. What's left over will likely be a debt you'll carry to your grave and pass on to your survivors. You've got to understand, we're talking major bucks here. Hospitals are not cheap. Doctors are not cheap. And miracles are darn near exorbitant."

He slipped a business card out of his pocket and tossed it onto the rolling meal table to my left. Over Lenny's left shoulder a contestant overbid and Hans the Cliff Climbing Yodeler fell off the price mountain. A tuba blatted out a losers' theme. I looked at Scum of the Earth and then at his business card laying on the fake wood grain surface of the roll-away table and thought that the price is wrong, Mr. Lawyer Man, thanks for playing but the price is wrong.

"And what I told my cousin and what I would tell you, Mr. Johnston, is that there *is* a cost and someone, like it or not, will have to pay. But that person doesn't *have* to be you. And why should it be? In my experience, the blame for such an incident is rarely the sole possession of the injured."

For a split second I saw the ladder. I could almost feel the shifty steps.

"And so the question is, 'Who's to blame?'"

"I am." Miss Rosie stood in my doorway, a Shop-Rite brown paper sack clutched in her arm. I had no idea how long she had been there or how much she had heard. "I'm to blame," she said and if I'm not mistaken, I think her lower lip quivered ever so slightly before she firmed up. "Now get out of my best friend's room. It's time for his breakfast."

That swingy Price is Right music gave way to the silence before the first commercial and in that brief moment, the two of them faced-off, the old lady and the ambulance chaser. At last, the old lady won. Leonard Gay, who had been called numerous things in his lifetime but will always be Scum of the Earth to me, nodded in my direction and made for the door where there was another mini-standoff before the foot-and-a-half shorter Miss Rosie pivoted on a heel and allowed the lawyer to leave, smiling as slickly as when he entered.

Miss Rosie came on in and as she set the paper bag on the meal table (I could smell something hot, probably a stack of her strawberry waffles), her eyes drifted over to my visitor's business card. I was telling her good morning and asking what's for breakfast and how was her drive in, but she wasn't listening; she was thinking. Finally, I caught on to what she was looking at and a wave of sudden embarrassment flooded through me. I had just opened my mouth to explain that she had absolutely positively nothing to worry about, that I would never think of filing a suit against her, that she could ball that fancy business card up and chunk it in the toilet and flush for all I cared when she slipped the card into the front pocket of her elastic-waist denim pants and held up a finger.

"I'll be just right back."

Then she jogged back out of the room, the appetizing aroma of a fresh warm homemade breakfast churned and mixed in the air with her ever-present perfume, the kind the new generation call "Grandmama Musk". I heard her footfalls fade away down the hall and I thought I heard her call out for Mr. Gay before she passed completely out of earshot. My curiosity bent my attention around my door and past the nurses station but no matter how hard I tried all I could hear was the *bl-bl-ble-ble-ble-bleep-bleep...bleep...bleep* of Barker's massive showdown wheel coming from the forgotten television. By the time I won my fumbling thumb-wrestling match with the remote control and had the volume on the TV set down to a near-mute level, there was nothing to hear but the soft shuffling *squeak-pad* sounds of Miss Rosie's white low-top Keds on their return trip, the hospital's shiny white tile flooring frequently swept and buffed. Then she wheeled back into the room, her face bearing the gratified expression of someone having just completed a task that turned out to be easier than anticipated.

She surprised me by clapping her hands together loudly. "Now," she said opening the paper sack and unloading Tupperware, "I bet you are starved." I peeked as she began opening the containers and smiled when I saw I was right about the strawberry waffles. Also, there were cheese-smothered scrambled eggs, smoking patties of sausage, home-fried potatoes, and a thermos of chilled orange juice. As she was preparing the food, I grabbed the remote and returned the TV to a reasonable volume. It was just in time for one of Bob's signature moments, a joke followed by a true gen-u-wine chuckle and a wink, and the studio audience roared.

"Now there," Miss Rosie said, her back to the television, her hands busy opening cartons, "is a man with real class."

I tried to hide my smile but couldn't and when she looked at me we shared in a moment of brief bubbly laughter. Then she sat down in the bedside chair and, even though I was perfectly able to do it myself, she began to feed me breakfast.

twenty

The phone had a sticker that read **Dial "0" for Hospital Operator or "9 + Number" for Outbound Calls** so I punched nine and quickly dialed. It rang only twice.

"Hello?"

"Hey Tiff, it's Eric. You busy?"

She exhaled like you do when you sit down, especially when you sit on something soft, like a sofa.

"No, not busy," she said. Her voice was guarded to be sure, but not nearly as walled off as the previous time we spoke on the telephone. I had hardly the time to say "hello" last Autumn before Tiffany's desire to end the conversation was as subtly apparent as an overly lit billboard on the freeway. Perhaps being almost-dead had an upside. "Just doing a few little things around the house. How are you, Eric?"

"I'm okay. Well, not *okay-okay*, but getting better."

"Are they telling you anything?"

"They tell me lots of things. Too many, really. But the gist of it all is that I should be able to go home soon-*ish*. As soon as they feel confident that the swelling has gone down as far as it can."

"Oh, okay. That sounds...good, I think."

"Yeah, yeah. I think it's good news."

This was where the conversation began to turn toward the awkward. Suddenly, it was floundering on the brink of a strained silence.

"Hey Tiff, I was wondering if you'd be okay with bringing Megan by for another visit. It was really great to see her, both of you, the other day and I thought maybe we could do it again."

"Well...Eric..."

She was about to say no.

"The cafeteria here is really something to see, Tiff. They have this thing called an ice cream machine and there are these funny coney looking things you can put the ice cream in and everything. Megan would absolutely love it. In fact, I'm not sure she would forgive you if you deprive her of such quality ice cream. You know a grudge like that could follow her well into adulthood..."

"Eric, stop it. The reason we came by the other day was as a favor to your friend, Rosie Cotcher. I'm not saying it was a bad thing, you seeing Megan, and I'm not saying it won't happen again, but I just don't want your hopes getting too high."

Hopes too high, I thought. Hopes too high? For a moment, my anger flared. My face tightened down and my skin got hot. I wanted to see my daughter. *My* daughter, and here was someone warning me not to get my hopes too high. Then I was slammed with the memory of what I had done and with the immediacy of a fire extinguisher, I chilled out.

"I understand," I replied evenly.

"I'm just saying that you need to focus on you right now. Get better. Get home. The rest will work itself out."

Or it won't, I thought, but I kept that thought to myself. That kind of negativity would only sour the entire offer. I had put myself out there and I didn't want to become a sore looser.

"Okay. Well, I guess that's it, isn't it?"

"I guess so. Oh, wait. One more thing, Eric. Would you mind doing me a favor and tell Miss Rosie that Megan and I said hello and that she's welcome to drop back by again? At tea-time. Say that; she'll know what it means." And then she added, "I'd appreciate it."

I said I would and then I hung up the phone.

twenty-one

"Quick, pick your feet up."

I looked down at Miss Rosie with a half-grin, half-smirk, you-really-think-you're-funny type of expression on my face. Since the accident, I hadn't done anything with my feet, including all things "quick".

"Well, by golly, use your hands to help if you need them," she said. "Just hustle a little bit would you?"

I cupped a hand under my knee and lifted.

"No, NO. *Both* of them at the same time. Now come on let's go."

There was a slap as my bare foot came back down on the metal wheelchair footrest. It probably would have hurt if my feet were in the hurting business. As I reached down with both hands and scooped my legs up, I asked her what gives? What's the big rush?

Miss Rosie slid a fluffed pillow beneath my raised feet and I released my hold. I couldn't quite feel the pillow, but there was a faint sponginess in my hips and knee joints, like surfing on a cloud. After placing the pillow, Miss Rosie worked on standing up, taking the endeavor in three major acts: getting to a single knee, pushing off, and straightening. For a moment she seemed dizzy. Her eyes swam and she placed a hand to her forehead. When I reached toward her to provide support, which could be deemed laughable considering I had only recently regained the function of my upper extremities and was currently struggling with the lower two, she slapped my hand away.

"We are hurrying, Mr. Johnston, because we don't have much time. Jeremy will pop in any minute now and I want to give something a try before he shows up."

Then she came around behind me and wheeled me to the foot of my bed, facing the window. I heard her kick down the wheelchair brakes and then she circled around in front of me and launched herself up onto the bed like a swimmer coming out of a pool. Then she put her arms out in front of her like a mummy's but with clenched fists like she was gripping an invisible something.

"I think this will work better if you don't look down, Mr. Johnston."

I looked at her in a state of dubiety and asked her if she would repeat her previous statement. She was heading somewhere and I wasn't following.

"Don't look down," she said, over-pronouncing each word as if hearing them was the issue and understanding them was a given. "At your feet. And put your hands up on the yoke."

I did as I was told, but as I raised my arms in my own mummy-esque pose, I told her it would be easier for me to play along if I knew what it was we were doing.

"I'm wondering if Jeremy's not going about this whole thing wrong. His aim is for you to walk. Nothing wrong with that. Or maybe there is. See, I think you'd rather fly. So," she took a deep breath and resituated her hands on her imaginary flight controls, "if you've got to crawl before you can walk, you've got to taxi before you fly. And that's what we're doing, Mr. Johnston. Taxiing. So check your flaps and throttle up."

I sat for a minute and tried to think of all the reasons that this was ridiculous. I imagined Jeremy or anyone else walking into my room and catching us, a middle aged man and an elderly woman, in the midst of a serious game of make-believe. Then I looked down at my lifeless feet and remembered looking down at my hands not too long ago. I remembered the day Miss Rosie had tricked my arms into working and suddenly all the reasons not to do as she asked seemed small and empty. I twisted left and I twisted right, then I pulled out on the throttle before floating my hands on the yoke.

I told her the flaps looked good, throttle was out, and we were moseying up the taxiway.

"Good. Now, this baby's got nose-wheel controls patched into the pedals and braking set up on a differential. And there's quite a bit of ground clutter out here today so you better be sharp on your turns, Mr. Johnston." She pointed up ahead. "Oh, here we go. Let's miss this luggage truck. Easy turn to the left. Keep an eye on that right wing."

It went on like that for quite a while. Miss Rosie would call out obstacles and I would try to miss them, never looking down and never knowing if I was truly in control of our invisible aircraft. But after every quote-unquote turn, Miss Rosie would toss me a "good job" or an offhand comment on how narrowly we missed the previous hinderance, always by just the skin of our teeth or a kitty-whisker. And before long, as is customary with the best games of make-believe, I began to lose myself. I became so engrossed in my maneuvering around cargo trucks, hangars, and other aircrafts that I barely noticed the spongy sensation travel down from my hips to my knees to my ankles and finally to the tips of my toes. I was too busy taxiing our plane to take stock of the fact that I was moving my feet.

"Alright," Miss Rosie said after countless close encounters, "looks like we've made it to the runway. Let's come to a full stop on my mark and...Now!"

I pressed my toes down into the pillow hard, pushing its fluff out towards its edges. I pushed hard enough to feel the footrests beneath the pillow's softness. I pushed hard enough for it to hurt, but it was a good hurt. I looked down at my feet and shook my head in slow wonder. Then I looked back up through my window and, for the first time in months, allowed myself the hope of flying again.

twenty-two

During the next five days, everything happened quickly.

I began to walk. It took an hour of Jeremy checking and rechecking the pressure I could apply with my leg muscles to convince him to let me try. It was the first time I'd seen genuine uncertainty on his typically cocky face but I knew it immediately for what it was; the worry of expected failure. He didn't think I could do it and he was scared of the psychological repercussions of an unsuccessful attempt. But eventually and without his usual motivational/threatening spiel, he wheeled me up to the parallel bars and lifted me with his hands under my armpits to a standing position. Such was his lack of faith in my ability, I felt a strong inclination to make him sweat out a few more tense moments, but that notion was fleeting. I smiled as childishly as I could muster and cast a wink at my young pony-tailed trainer before scissor-stepping awkwardly between the bars first in one direction then back the way I'd come. When I got back to my chair, panting and sweating in cold sheets but feeling better than I had in months if not years, Jeremy was one split-face joker-mask of a grin and two wildly pumping fists.

I was even stronger the next day. My occupational therapy transitioned to include activities requiring the function of my upper *and* lower extremities. I relearned how to clean myself on a toilet, how to put on a pair of jeans, and a dozen other tasks most people, including myself not eight months before, take completely for granted.

And, of course, I walked. And walked. When I got tired of walking in a straight line, Jeremy had me walk in circles or up a short flight of stairs. We walked down the hallways, we walked through the cafeteria, the lobby, the doctors' lounge. We walked around the parking lot. Often, we would gather a following. Small knots of hospital employees, fellow patients, visitors, clergy-folk. They would walk along with us down a stretch of hallway or up a floor or a lap or two around the exterior of the building and they would listen to Jeremy's recitation of my progress report and they would provide encouragement. They would smile and pat me gently on the back and speak of miracles and God's providential care. I would smile back and nod and thank them for their kind words and just keep on pumping my feet. And for the next several days, with each and every step, I grew stronger and more confident.

Then came the doctor parade. Each would knock curtly on the door as they swept into my room, provide some form of physical inspection - the reflexes of the knee, a penlight into the eyes to check pupil dilation, stethoscope to the ribcage, you name it - flip through my chart, mutter beneath their breath, and leave. The only muttering I was able to understand was a vague mention of discharge which I took to indicate my impending departure from the hospital and not the leakage of any bodily fluids as I currently had none. The caboose of the doctor train was none other than Granville. Doctor "Maybe" himself. He stopped in just long enough to pat me chummily on the shoulder and say, "Told you we'd fix you right up, didn't I?"

Finally, word was passed down that I could leave. Vamoose, scoot, skedaddle. When the nurse told me the news, I instinctively turned toward the chair I had come to think of as Miss Rosie's only to find it empty. In fact, as I thought about it, Miss

Rosie had been absent for the past week or so. I had been too busy with my milestones of achievement to notice the lack of Price is Right and the abundance of flavorless powdered egg breakfasts in the mornings. As this realization hit home, my heart became a cardiac yo-yo, dropping suddenly to an area around my knees and then rising past its normal anatomical position and into my throat, beating in fluttering trios that made my head swim like a balloon taped to a popsicle stick.

As my eyes were filled with a blurred image of her empty chair, my mind ran through countless scenarios, each resulting in the demise of a small crotchety woman with the three-fold burden of loneliness, advanced age, and an inoperable brain tumor. And then the shuffling visions stopped and I settled on one. It seemed so horrifically clear. She'd stroked out, a banana-shaped sliver of her tumor no bigger than a fraction of a millimeter in length had broken off and lodged itself in one of the tiny capillaries of her brain. Blood flow was occluded. The area of her brain fed by that particular capillary began to starve and die. The right side of her body went slack in the span of two seconds, spilling her onto the brown linoleum of her kitchen floor. The age-weakened capillary burst and the nickel-sized portion of her brain that was thirsting for a meager sip of nutrient-rich lifeblood was now drowning in it and dying all the faster because of it. A string of spit made contact with the linoleum and a single rogue thought of her mop and bucket standing in the back corner of the mud room tumble-weeded through her ebbing cognitive center just before she lost her grasp on consciousness forever. She was laying there stroked out on her kitchen floor, the refrigerator door swung open, its light blaring and sucking electricity that will be billed to her estate, a bowl of cut strawberries meant for my waffles broken into shards at her feet, its contents splayed out around her like red fruit rose-buds. She was laying there dead with no one to find her until she missed her Sunday School or I phoned Nora Jo and Glenn.

Call Glenn. There might be time.

I reached over to the phone, one hand seizing the receiver and the other punching out nine plus the number just like the sticker commanded when I happened to glance up at the discharge nurse. A flash of something red just over her white-clad shoulder caught my eye. I put the phone back down and calmly waited for the nurse to step aside. When she did, she revealed a beaming, conscious, cognizant, and very much alive Miss Rosie Cotcher. I considered asking her if she was aware that she had very nearly killed me via a massive coronary event but then her smile widened even larger and I forgot all about berating her. She folded her hands into a triumphant knot beneath her chin.

"Home, Mr. Johnston," she said. "Home."

twenty-three

Home had become a little place called Millwood Branch. I had lived in lots of different places, most of them for a longer stretch of time than I had been in the Bakers' house on Main Street, but that made little difference. Some unknown soul long ago prosed that home is where the heart is and no matter how long I may have lived in sunny Florida, suburban East Memphis, or Methodist Hospital, my heart was nestled in the smooth rolling hills of Hickahala County.

I said goodbye to my room, although it was no longer technically my room. Currently, it was the hospital's room and within the hour it would be lent out to someone else. Someone I had never met, someone who had absolutely no idea or reason to care about what I had been through within this room's four white walls. My smell had already vacated, replaced by the sterile tinge of isopropyl alcohol. The bedding had been changed. It felt more like saying goodbye to an acquaintance than an old worn-in friend, but I said it nonetheless, aloud, and pulled the door closed behind me.

As I walked down the hallway, I took the opportunity to marvel at my progress. I had entered Methodist unconscious, unable to breathe of my own accord, my body as broken as a twig snapped in two. Now I was walking out of the same door the paramedics had wheeled my gurney through those many months before, fully capable of living a complete life. Even the white straight-line scar down the back of my neck would be easily concealed by the collar of my pilot shirts. And it was just as I was reflecting on these things, the mighty journey I had traveled back from the brink of life itself, that I heard the soft pat-pat sound of gentle applause and was suddenly reminded of the fact that I had not made that journey alone.

The automatic doors whooshed open and I was greeted by the pleasant warming rays of the southern sunshine and two lines of cheering hospital employees, each grinning from ear to ear. There was the ICU nurse, Rick, his bald head gleaming. There was the charge nurse from my floor and the overnight nurse whom I barely recognized in the brightness of the day through my fully-awake eyes. The pharmacists that had managed my IV feedings were there, too. Janitors, and the ladies from the linens service, and X-ray techs, and nurses I couldn't remember, and even the lunch orderlies, including the poor young man Miss Rosie had threatened with her plastic flatware. And of course the Doctor Parade. As I passed down the center of the two lines, some called out words of encouragement over the din of applause, some scurried out of formation and embraced me, whispering congratulatory nothings in my ear.

Jeremy was at the end of the line. His face was full of vehemence.

"Was it hard?"

I didn't hesitate. "The absolute hardest thing I've ever done. Ever."

His face broke open in a grin and he bear-hugged me, lifting my feet off the concrete walkway. "Good," he said in my ear. "That's good. Then everything else should be easy." And then he set me down, gripped my hand in a crushing one-shake-handshake, and resumed his place in line, clapping along with the rest of them.

Dr. Granville was next and instead of extending his right hand for a shake, he smiled impishly and held out a pair of scissors. After a moment of confusion, I caught his meaning. The applause swelled as I rolled up my sleeve and allowed the doctor to snip off my hospital identification bracelet. I turned back to the crowd and waved it over my head jokingly and their cheers swelled again. When I turned back to Granville, he was holding a familiar object out to me.

"We thought this would make an even better keepsake, Mr. Johnston," he said as I took the metal halo from him and the cheers rose to their loudest. It felt light in my hands and I resisted the sudden urge to hurl it out across the parking lot and watch it like a stone skipping across a pond. Instead, I thanked him and then turned back to the crowd and mouthed thanks to the collective.

At the very end of the line was Miss Rosie's Chrysler. I opened the passenger-side door, waved a final goodbye, and ducked inside. Miss Rosie looked over at me from her seat behind the wheel.

"Ready?"

I looked down at the halo in my lap. The emotion of the moment caught up with me and my vision began to blur. A moment passed and I breathed in large gulps of free non-hospital air and fought off the impulse to break down into sobs.

"Mr. Johnston?"

"Yes ma'am," I said, pulling myself together and blinking away the uncried tears. "Ready."

And we left. It was an overwhelmingly beautiful day and an equally gorgeous drive. After the white-wash of the hospital, the earth's natural greens and blues were vivid and attention-demanding. We took the trip in almost absolute silence. Had I known it was the last time I would have to talk with her, I would

have. I would have picked her brain about her youth, or the latest
gossip about town, or flying, or anything. But of course, I didn't.
The Chrysler bore me smoothly home and we were both content
to absorb the landscape individually, without interruption from
the other.

twenty-four

I didn't sleep well that first night.

I laid in my own bed, my very own smooth pillow beneath my head, and looked up into the darkness. The Bakers' house was exactly as I had left it. The living room was uncluttered and precise; the remote controls, the *Bi-planes of the 1920s* coffee table book, the reading lamp, everything was perfectly in its place with only the slightest sheet of dust as evidence of my extended absence. There was a batch of folded clothes in a basket on the dryer. The kitchen counters were bare, each plate and pot and pan in its appointed place in the cabinets. My bed was still made. It looked oddly solid and immoveable, as if it had been there in that spot for a hundred years and would remain there for a hundred more. Below and around it, the bedroom carpet still showed lines from the last time I vacuumed. Someone had driven my I'd-rather-be-flying KIA home and placed it in the garage. I had stared at it for a long time, at last deciding that although it looked vastly different than I remembered, it was in fact mine.

I was home and surrounded by all the right things in all the right places. The house's central unit had kept chugging right along while I was gone, keeping the place within a normal range of temperatures, not to mention unstale, so my insomnia that first night could not be laid at its ancient feet. Even the crickets were doing their part, chirping a deep south lullaby outside my bedroom window.

There I laid, swaddled in all the organized comfort I had made for myself, and I could not drift off on the wings of sleep. I unlaced my fingers and let my hand fall onto the other side of the bed. There was so much space over there, more than twice as much as I had had on my hospital bed the previous night. I extended my arm and felt the vast emptiness beside me. It was cold and I'm not sure the Bakers' old AC unit could be wholly blamed for that either.

As I laid there blinking up at the ceiling, one hand on my heart and the other slowly caressing the vacant sheets, my thoughts turned to Tiffany. I drew a picture of her in my mind. She was wearing one of my old t-shirts she used to sleep in and had just removed her makeup and she was laying herself down on the bed, there in the cold empty space beside me, her long red hair spilling its auburn strands on the satin-covered pillow. She was smiling at me, not just with her mouth and lips but also with her eyes, and I thought I'd never seen a more beautiful thing. She nestled her head, still looking at me, and slipped her arm under the pillow like she always did.

For a moment, I just looked at my fabricated apparition and wondered if she ever ran her hand over my side of the bed and was shocked at the sheets' cruel coolness. To my surprise, I hoped she didn't. It was a change in my thinking but it was genuine. I hoped that our old house was as messy and devoid of my obsessiveness as possible. I hoped Tiffany was fast asleep, having listened to the soft even breaths of our daughter on the baby monitor until slumber over-swept her. And mostly, I hoped she wasn't thinking of me. I hoped she was happy.

And at last, my eyelids slid together, and I sailed away.

twenty-five

The doorbell.

My eyes came open and I was immediately lost. Without moving, my senses cast around, gathering clues of my whereabouts and with each gathered one, the default image of my little room in Methodist Memorial was dissolved and washed down the mental drain-grate at the bottom of my memory.

The sheet beneath me was not coarse enough. The bed was too parallel with the floor and I was nestled down inside its pillow-top too comfortably. The walls were not alabaster white, but rather a deep soothing chocolate. The sunlight was muted more by curtains than by the horizontal lines of cheap blinds. The air smelled fresh with the slightest hint of honeysuckle.

I gave it a moment to register, my heart beating madly inside my rib cage in the sudden surge of adrenaline. And still I was lost.

Again, the doorbell.

The realization that I was home drenched me like a bucket of cold water and I was relieved to feel the hammering in my chest slow to a more normal rhythm. I sat up in the bed and swung my legs over the side. My toes were wiggling and I took a moment to smile down at them. Then, I yawned and stretched and swiped the crust from the corners of my eyes. The sunlight peeking around the edge of my curtain had a downward slant and a decisively late-morning-early-afternoon quality about it and I quickly realized that I had overslept. I was just musing to myself about exactly what I had overslept since I had absolutely nothing to do, except of course to get my life back on track after a six months hiatus, when the sound of the doorbell again cut through the house, this time followed by an impatient series of knuckle-raps on the glass panes of the front door.

I shouted that I was on my way and muttered something to myself about keeping your pants on as I stalked sleepily over to my closet to find a pair of my own. I pulled on a pair of jeans I hadn't laid eyes on since before last Christmas, again cognizant of the fact that I was unable to accomplish such a difficult four-limbed maneuver two weeks prior, and a t-shirt from an old summer softball league. The doorbell rang again and I padded barefoot on the hardwood, down the hallway towards the front door, muttering all the while about patience, patience, patience.
I jerked the door open and blinked confusedly into the blaring sunshine. At first, I thought my eyes were deceiving me, that they were still asleep, but nothing changed as they gradually adjusted to the nearly overwhelming light. There on my doorstep, fully equipped with his slightly off-center lawyerly smile and combed straight back hair, stood Leonard Buford Gay, Attorney at Law and Scum of the Earth.

"Mr. Johnston, hello," he said, his hand coming up flat from his side. I ignored it as I had when we were first acquainted. After a moment, he allowed it to swing back down, unshaken. But that moment seemed to drag on and on and within it, we looked at one another. God and Leonard only knew how much shock and repulsion was expressed on my face as even I was momentarily disconnected. "Might I come in, Mr. Johnston?"

Again my mind flashed on Count Dracula and the dangers of inviting him into your home. Not to mention a million likely quips comparing blood-sucking vampires to blood-sucking lawyers. However, I remained speechless, for once following the age-old adage of "if you have nothing nice to say, say nothing at all".

"Mr. Johnston," he continued in a leveled, no-nonsense tone, "I know what you must think of me; I am not an ignorant person. And I am certainly familiar with the disgusted look that's on your face right now. But please rest assured that I am not here to argue in favor of the merits of my work. Nor am I here to harass you or proposition you or solicit your business. I have news and we have matters to discuss and I think it would be better dealt with inside. So I would greatly appreciate it if you might place your hatred of me on hold for a moment and allow me in."

After a moment's contemplation, I stepped to one side and let him in. His sports jacket smelled like mothballs as he passed under my nose and into the front parlor. I shut the door and gestured for him to sit, which he did, appearing utterly out of place on my comfy charcoal-gray sofa. I sat silently in the love seat opposite him and waited. Leonard Gay crossed his legs, picked at a ball of fuzz on his sock, and then quickly put both feet back on the floor. Finally, he started.

"Do you remember the day we first met, Mr. Johnston? At the hospital?"

I said I did, of course.

"Do you remember that Miss Cotcher...Miss Rosie, if I might, caught up with me after I left your room that day?"

I said yes, I remembered.

"Did she ever talk to you about our conversation, Mr. Johnston?"

I said that no, she didn't, and I asked if he would kindly get to the point.

Again, Lenny crossed and uncrossed his legs. He looked about as comfortable as a kitten on a metal table.

"The point," he mumbled, "yes, the point." Then he collected himself and blew out a long breath and looked me square in the eyes. "Mr. Johnston, I regret to inform you that Rosie Cotcher passed this early morning."

I remember repeating the word "passed", such an odd way of putting it.

"Yes," he said. "Passed away."

At that moment, I began to float as if in a dream. I watched and listened from above my head, but I couldn't feel my hands dry washing in my lap or my eyes blinking through the gathering tears. I could hear my voice asking about the how's and the when's from down below like the voice of someone shouting up from a basement, but I have no recollection of choosing or forming the words.

"It happened sometime in her sleep. And you would be glad to know she was found laying peacefully in her bed. A stroke, they think it was. That seems to be eventual cause of death for most folks with her particular condition."

I must have looked at him questioningly.

"Yes, yes, she told me about the cancer. And a great deal more, too. In fact, Miss Rosie and I have been in almost constant correspondence these past few weeks since our first meeting. There was much work to be done and unfortunately, it seems we were correct to make haste."

Again, I must have looked at him questioningly. He held up a finger and produced a thin briefcase I hadn't noticed he had brought in and set it delicately on the coffee table. The clasps popped open loudly in the unsettling silence and I unconsciously flinched.

"You may have noticed that Miss Rosie was more frequently absent during your final weeks of recovery at Methodist. It was not because she didn't care. As a matter of fact, it was quite the contrary." He began pulling out stacks of forms, forms of various colors and worded in all manner of legalese, most bearing the scrawled signature of Rosie Cotcher near the bottom. "She sold her land, all but what the house sits on, back to James Sebastian

Settlemires. Also, she held an auction and sold off most of her furniture, her sewing machine, her recipes. And with that money, plus the bulk of her life savings..." Here he whipped out one final form and the floating me above my head could just make out the words Methodist Memorial and Eric Johnston and Zero Balance. "She paid your bill. Every dime."

Some distant part of my mind staggered at this awesome display of generosity. No one had ever gone so far to make sure my needs were met. Under different circumstances, it would have been cause for celebration, smiles and back slapping and toasts in honor of such a great deed of selflessness, but instead, my heart lifted only a little. If I'd had the choice, I would have traded that receipt of payment and that mountain of debt for more time with my friend, even for just one more relaxing conversation over a slice of caramel pie.

My fingers wiped wetness from the corners of my eyes and into the ribbed denim of my jeans. I sniffed and cleared my throat, noticing that I was becoming less and less numb, more in control of my voluntary self. There was still something odd about the entire situation and I wanted to figure it out before the moment had passed. And so, through the fading wisps of mental fogginess, I tried to be polite as I asked Leonard Buford Gay why him? Why was he involved?

"Well, from her point of view, I had the expertise to draw up any necessary contracts and to ensure the legality of each transaction, not to mention that I'm an out-of-towner and could be relied upon to keep her secret close to the chest. For my part, believe it or not, I am a man of principles. The just thing, as I recall alluding to in your hospital room, was for her to pay your medical expenses. She was eager to do so and, court or no court, I was willing to help."

I nodded, slowly seeing Leonard Gay in a totally new light, an uncomfortably stiff little man in a tan mothball-smelling sports jacket. A man who was once a boy with a mother that hadn't cared enough to put braces on that slightly shifted smile, a boy who was undoubtably ridiculed at school and had vowed to prove them all wrong. Suddenly, Scum of the Earth seemed too harsh a title for him and I felt a momentary rush of shame for the way I had thought of him with such a small pool of experience from which to draw. As if to make amends, I offered him a cup of coffee. I couldn't vouch for its freshness as it had sat untouched in my pantry for these past six months, but I thought there was enough to make a pot. He shook his head.

"I can't stay," he said, slipping a white envelope from the briefcase and then lowering the lid and clasping it closed. "There is just one more thing. Miss Rosie placed a single conditional requirement on the payment to the hospital. It won't go completely through until it has been satisfied. She said that you made a promise and that she wouldn't have you breaking your word."

As he told me what I had to do, I felt a grin spread across my face. Fresh tears warmed my cheeks. I listened in silence and couldn't help but marvel at her. Even in death she had found a way to get things done. When he finished, he handed me the envelope and I walked him to the door. We shook hands for the first time and he left.

twenty-six

I drove out Bullfrog Road. I heard the loose gravel ping the KIA's undercarriage. I watched the green finger of Old Man Settlemires's silo pass outside my window. I turned in. I parked in Miss Rosie's driveway.

I found the spare key under the same old brick. I let myself in. I smelled the last bit of her baking still thick in the air. I circled the empty sitting room. I ran a finger along the paneling wall. I stared at the imprint her sewing machine had left in the carpet.

I sat Indian style in the floor and I opened the envelope and I read her words.

Dear Mr. Johnston,

I trust this letter finds you well.

First, there's no need for any nonsense sadness. However it happened, you had better believe that I'm glad it's over and done with so any tears you may shed will be on your own behalf, not mine. So that's final.

Next. I assume Mr. Gay has told you everything. I would apologize for keeping our dealings secret from you if I wasn't entirely sure it was the right thing to do, but it was. You were getting better by leaps and bounds (and still are, I hope) and you needed to focus on you. All of this would have been distracting for you whether you'd admit it or not. It was *the right thing to do.* I stand by that.

Speaking of Mr. Gay. He's not a bad person. He may be city (remember where you came from?) and he may be a little off, but he's not bad. In fact, he's been a great help to me (and you too if you think about it) and you should be nice to him.

Next. My house will be donated to the church to be used as a parsonage. As a favor, I hope you wouldn't mind showing Gene and Nora Jo around the place? Thanks.

Next. Here I must apologize for I am truly sorry for your injury. If you only knew the nights I laid sleepless thinking of the damage I'd caused you. I want you to know I burned my grandaddy's ladder, the one you toppled from. I doused it in too much gasoline and it went up in a fireball so high somebody driving by (probably one of them pulpwood truck-drivers) called the volunteer fire department. It was quite a sight. But I know that no amount of ashes and no amount of money can ever make what happened to you right. And for that, again I am sorry. So so sorry.

Next and last. I must confess another secret. You know now of my meetings with Leonard Gay and the reason for all the hush-hush, but I've been an even busier bee than you think. I have also visited with your wife, Tiffany on several occasions. And of course your lovely daughter, Megan (she serves me the most delicious imaginary tea from a little plastic tea set, so cute!). And yes it was me that convinced Ms. Tiffany not to visit you in the hospital frequently (that one time in the rec room was an emergency situation, you understand) so do not hold that against her. If anything, she wanted to go and see about you, but she was willing to heed my advice. As for why, I could never even begin to explain where you would understand. It would be like explaining a woman's soul and I believe we both know that cannot be done. But I hope it comes to you someday and when it does, remember this one final piece of advice: whatever you think you should say, whatever you think you should do, ball it up and throw it in the trash and just apologize. Don't make any ex-

cuses and CERTAINLY don't make any of your stupid little jokes. Just *apologize.*

Godspeed,

Rosie

p.s. As for your conditional requirement, Mr. Johnston, there's one of my grandaddy's old maps in the chest out in the shed's attic (I believe you know all too well where that chest is, don't you?). It should help.

And that was it.

I refolded the letter and put it back inside the envelope. I leaned my back against the wall and I watched the dust motes float lazily in the window-light. I got up. I locked the door behind me. I put the key back under the brick.

I ducked back into the KIA and I drove home.

twenty-seven

I set up a mental and emotional blockade around myself and slipped through the next two days. Nothing got past my defenses, nothing penetrated. I went through the acts necessary for life, I drew breath, I ate, I drank, I slept, but everything else was kept at an arm's distance. Even thoughts of Tiffany and Megan which had developed into hallucinations with such vividness they could almost be touched and felt, came to me only in passing and were quickly shooed away by the armada surrounding my inner self. In a word, I was numb.

The second day after Miss Rosie's death, I toured Gene and Nora Jo around her house and grounds. I pointed out the age-old homemade bricks that served to demarcate the patch of front yard from the flower beds. Nora Jo must have sensed my disconnected state and sympathized because she refrained from her typical chattery nature and simply nodded her head and promised the bricks would stay.

I showed them inside the house and was glad to see that when I slipped off my shoes and placed them on the front doorstep out of habit, they both followed suit without so much as a questioning expression. We walked through each of the rooms, our sock-feet whispering each step respectfully on Miss Rosie's carpet. They were very polite, the preacher and his wife, but honestly, it wouldn't have mattered if they hadn't been. At each stop, at the kitchen, the guest room, the coat closet, they would smile and say how suitable everything was, but like I said, I was numb. If they had thrown their hands up and shouted obscenities I wouldn't have flinched.

When we had finished with the house, I offered to walk the grounds with Gene. We slipped back into our shoes and left Nora Jo sitting placidly on the front porch. The chain supporting the two-seater swing gave tiny familiar whines as she swung ever so slightly. She already looked at home, her face bearing a handsomely soft smile in the early morning light.

The dew was still thick on the grass, pearls and glittering diamonds on a sea of deep emerald, and our shoes collected grass clippings as we cut across the yard to the corner of the property. I pointed out the corner post and drew an imaginary line with my finger toward the back marker near the tree line, indicating the place where Leonard Gay and Old Man Settlemires had agreed to split the land. Then we strolled through the wet grass into the back yard.

"I gave up the drink."

Gene's voice was clear and strong but it was different from his preaching voice; it was more personal, more honest. He was being the real him which wasn't necessarily the preaching him. Still, my reaction was blunted. I simply furrowed my brows and stabbed my hands down into my pockets and continued to stroll.

"I used to drink. Even recently, I'm ashamed to admit. I wasn't a happy person and alcohol was my means of escape. But that's too close to an excuse and there truly is no excuse for my behavior. Anyway, I gave it all up. *Trying* to give it all up."

I began to realize that Gene was baring his soul to me and although my emotional armada was still in place, it allowed a transient moment of weakness, a single ship bearing supplies to sail through the impenetrable blockade of warships.

I told Gene in short choppy sentences that I used to have the same problem. That I let it take me too far. That I allowed the alcohol to push me away from the things in my life that were irreplaceable. That we were quite nearly in the same shoes. That I was still struggling to get my own life back on track. And that I would help him, that we could help each other.

Gene smiled and nodded his head. A burden, it would seem, had been lifted. His face brightened and I could see that he was still a very young man. "That would be great," he said. "I-*we* would appreciate that." He cast a quick look back toward the house and Nora Jo and I realized something else: he loved her, and in no small amount. Then he laughed and said, "You know, Miss Rosie said I should talk about this with you, that you would understand and maybe help a little, and she was right."

But my old defenses were back up and I didn't let even the mention of her name soak in. I was numb again, unplugged and just going through the motions. And so we didn't say another word to one another until we reached the back shed.

As I slid the shed door open, a queer emotional wave engulfed me; I guess it was a combination of nostalgia, dread, and deja vu. I was reminded of the many mornings of the previous summer which would find me sliding open the same door to retrieve the chainsaw, of how strong and capable I had felt then. As if to aid in the forming of that memory, a waft of oil and saw dust, that aroma distinctive of old chainsaws, greeted Gene and me at the threshold.

My eyes were drawn to the patch of bare earth in the center of the shed. There was no unusual marking on that patch, no imprint or indentation, just bald, hard-packed dirt. Without realizing it, my hand came up to the back of my neck and my fingers traced the abnormally smooth line of the surgical scar there. For a moment, I drifted. I stared at the unaltered dirt floor of the shed and felt the place of my body that had been forever changed by it and I drifted.

Gene cleared his throat.

"She bought a new ladder," he said and gestured toward the back corner, the very same back corner which had been occupied by Miss Rosie's grandfather's tricky ladder for countless long years. My eyes followed his gesture into that corner and even in spite of the knowledge that she had destroyed the old wooden ladder in a towering inferno, I was shocked by its absence. A shiny metal ladder, never before used, gleamed back at me. Despite its reassuring newness, I measured it with a skeptical eye.

"Gene," I said, still sizing up the newfangled ladder, "I wonder if you might do me a favor."

"Sure," he responded willingly enough.

And so I told him what I needed. He didn't hesitate, in fact, he was moving for the ladder before I could even finish. This new ladder was much lighter and less cumbersome than the old one and Gene had it out of the corner and set up in place in no time flat. He placed a foot on its first rung just as I was finishing.

"And one more favor please, Gene," I said quickly.

He turned around, one foot on the ladder and one on that hard-packed patch of earth.

"Be careful." And then I let him do my favor.

twenty-eight

I spent the memorial service in my car.

It was the first real heat of the year so I cranked down my window and rolled up my sleeves, but I wouldn't get out. I had planned on getting out, of course, I had put on my sharpest tie and sports coat and practiced my repertoire of what I considered fitting funeral smiles in my bathroom mirror for no other purpose but to get out, but when that moment came, the moment that called for me to open the KIA's door and step out onto that gravel, onto that invisible but inevitable path that would lead me like a bridled pony to stand over her earthly remains, I could not do it.

At first, I struggled with myself, my hand on the door handle, but after a while the little man in my head that thought I could do it gave up and simply watched the black-clad mourners trickle into the church-house. There was the owner of Shop-Rite and his male friend. Before going into the church, they looked around cautiously and then straightened one another's ties and brushed the lint from the other's lapels. There was Doug Baxter from the local pharmacy. The high school principal and his young family scrambled out of their minivan and up to the open doors. The principal's foot caught the front of the first step and he nearly fell, stumbling for what seemed like minutes before finally regaining his balance. An unchecked burst of laughter emerged from my mouth and then I remembered where I was and the smile vanished. Everyone was there: the town lawmen, both current and retired, the aldermen, the mayor, waitresses and fry cooks from the Dairy Bar, the football coach, the hardware store owner, the shoe store owner, the town engineer, the town drunk. Everyone. Even the Methodist minister and her husband.

One of the last to arrive was J. Sebastian Settlemires, dressed in a brown Sunday jacket over a nice pair of overalls and leaning on his golden-handled cane. He looked diminutive plopping out of his oversized pick-up truck and crossing the parking lot. I wondered if he was happy to at long last have Miss Rosie's land, but to me, as he climbed the steps one by one and disappeared inside the church building, he didn't look happy. He just looked small and old and feeble.

I watched them all go into the church as I sat alone in my car and the sweat beaded up on my forehead. Then I watched as the funeral service director unclasped his hands and removed the wedges from under the church's front doors and slipped inside just before the hydraulic hinges sealed them all up. There was nothing more to see, so I looked down into my lap and eventually closed my eyes. For a while, all I could hear was the beat of my own pulse. Then, emerging from within the church, there came the sound of human voices singing that old gospel staple *How Great Thou Art*, softly at first, respectfully. Gradually, the volume swelled and there was passion dripping from each and every word. The song may have been muffled by the wood and rock of the church's walls but its melody and message were no less strong, no less true. After three stanzas, the singing stopped and I heard a general rumble as everyone inside sat back down on the unpadded pews. This was followed by a silence that stretched for nearly half an hour during which I imagined those gathered inside played witness to Gene's final farewell.

At last, the doors reopened. The wedges were put back into place. One by one, they began to leave. Everyone was so quiet. I could hear their shoes crunching the gravel of the parking lot but no one spoke above a whisper. Car doors slammed. Engines were cranked. More gravel was crunched as the lot began to empty. Excepting the funeral service staff, Gene and Nora Jo were the last to leave. The preacher led his wife to their car as she dabbed her eyes with a handkerchief, then they too were gone.

The parking lot was even quieter than before.

Suddenly, I felt like I needed to see her. The same impulse that had paralyzed me before now demanded action. I climbed out of the car and rushed to the church doors where I was met by the funeral director. As are all men that choose the field of mortuary sciences, he was an elderly gentleman with a lined face that seemed to be painted in a calm subtle smile. His arms were outstretched, directing me away from the entrance to the church, a seasoned rancher directing a stray steer.

"Sorry, son," he said. "Service is over. You just missed it."

He bent to remove the first of the two doorjamb wedges, but remained between me and the entrance. The left hand door swung shut with a whisper and a thud.

I said that I knew. That I knew the service was over and that I had missed the singing and speaking and shaking hands but that I just wanted to pay my respects.

"Ms. Cotcher is no longer available for viewing, son," he said, his face making spidery lines around his mouth that indicated sympathy, maybe even empathy.

I asked him what that was supposed to mean.

"It means she's not in there anymore."

I tried to look around him and down the middle aisle of the church but he shifted slightly to block my line of vision. I said that sure she was still there. The service only just now finished and I didn't see anyone wheel a casket out yet, so she had to still be in there.

"Took the body out the back, son," he said. "We only use the front doors if there's gonna be a graveside. I'm sorry but she's gone."

She's not gone, I told him. She's in there.

Then he put a hand on my shoulder.

"She's not. But even if she *was* still in there, she wouldn't be in there."

I searched the depths of his brown eyes for any hint of falsehood or insincerity and found none; he was telling the truth and now we both knew it. Still, I brushed his hand from my shoulder and roughed my way past him through the remaining open door. He called out for me to hold-up-now-son but otherwise put up very little resistance. I made it halfway up the aisle before the weight of everything landed on me. I think it was the tracks in the carpet, tracks from where they had wheeled her out, that finally pushed me over the emotional edge.

She was gone.

My friend was gone.

I began to cry.

I felt a hand squeeze my shoulder and I turned to face the funeral director again, that same tranquil expression on his shadow-creased face. He could have given me a tongue-lashing, could have told me in no uncertain terms to vacate the premises or ask me who the devil did I think I was, but he didn't. He didn't say a word and he didn't need to. He was right; she was gone, out the backdoor, but even if she hadn't been, she would be.

Gone.

After a moment, the old man pulled me in and I cried my tears onto his shoulder.

twenty-nine

The Bakers' house stayed dark that night.

I sat in the living room for a very long time. Nothing moved but my pupils adjusting to the meager light filtering in from the street and my chest rising and falling with each heavy breath. The crickets droned and the house settled; all else was silent. My sports jacket and tie lay in a wadded up crump on the adjacent sofa but even the compulsion to fold and hang, to prevent wrinkles, had been temporarily swept away by the recent tsunami of emotion.

If there had been liquor in the house, I would have poured myself a tall dry glass and kept the bottle close at hand. I hadn't touched the stuff since I let it drown my marriage, but I have no doubt I would have drank that night if for nothing else than to fill in the emptiness. But Hickahala County was and remains decidedly dry and the prospect of driving over to Littleton for a bottle or two only exhausted my already wearied mind.

I looked over at the phone, its outline barely visible in the gloom, and I thought about calling Tiffany. I saw myself picking up the receiver and dialing the numbers. It would ring twice, maybe three times, and she would pick up. We'd exchange hellos. The crickets would be droning on my end and the silence would buzz on hers and then what? I was in no shape to rehash the past and she would have little interest in consoling my grieving soul after what I had done to her. So then what?

Then nothing.

My thoughts turned to the day I left the hospital, not even a week prior. I remembered the roar of applause, the air of accomplishment, the warmth of a new beginning. I remembered the words with which Jeremy had left me and the assumption that everything else would be easy. Then I thought about those tracks in the church's carpet and the void inside the pit of my stomach echoed with sarcastic laughter. Easy was the way things were. Before the funeral. Before the accident. Before Millwood Branch. Before the infidelity.

But that was a lie, wasn't it? Casting a false nostalgic light on past events simply because they were beyond the reach of manipulation? The truth was it *hadn't* been easy then. Tolerable, enjoyable at times, but never easy. And how could any rational person ever assume the future would be any different?

I looked at the phone again but this time I knew I wouldn't pick it up. I wondered if I would ever pick it up again. Then a wave of fatigue swept over me and washed away all conscious thought and concern.

I got up slowly, my joints popping like dried twigs, and bunched my jacket up into a tighter ball at one end of the sofa. Then I laid down and went to sleep.

thirty

The next day was even hotter.

The KIA's radiator fan tinkered and whirred even after I'd killed the engine and stepped out into the sun's heat. Beyond the heat, my old friend humidity was back, transforming the act of breathing from what should be an involuntary task into a labor equivalent to pulling molasses up through a drinking straw. I squinted against the rising sun and examined the clapboard shack that served as flight control headquarters for the Littleton/Carr County Regional Airstrip. The front door stood open and I could see the spinning blades of oscillating fans inside. Papers on a large wooden desk caught the artificial breeze and rippled noisily. One such sheet of paper rippled high enough to get airborne and threatened to fly across the small room before a hand from behind the desk slapped it back down. An oily engine part, possibly a carburetor, was set down on top of the sheet of paper by a pair of equally oily hands.

I slammed my car door and the owner of the hands looked up from behind the desk.

"Morning mister," he said coming around the corner of the desk. He propped himself up in the doorway of the shack the way the gunfighters in every old Western flick ever made prop up in the doorways of saloons. He set his cap back on his head lazily. The name embossed on his shirt's iron-on tag read "Chuck".

I bid him a good morning.

Chuck looked at me, his eyebrows raised expectantly.

"Help ya?"

I pointed to the Cessna parked behind the shack on the edge of the runway and asked if it was his.

"Reckon you could say so," he answered. "Belongs to the strip and the strip belongs to me."

I told him it was a beautiful plane. Well taken care of.

"Yessir, I reckon that's no news to me."

I cleared my throat. Then I told Chuck I was there to charter the Cessna for the day if it was available for charter. Was it? Available for charter, that is? And I cleared my throat again.

Chuck pulled the brim of his cap back down and squinted at me. His eyes shifted over to my KIA and then back to me. I felt like a watermelon still on the vine and Chuck was playing the part of the seasoned farmer judging my ripeness.

"Reckon that depends, now don't it?"

I asked him on what exactly did it depend upon.

"Money, mostly," he said. "Ya got any?"

Just then we heard the rev of an engine and I turned to see a black German-engineered sportster leading a cloud of dust in our direction. The horn bleated out twice in short succession. I turned back toward Chuck and was unsurprised to see incredulity written on his grease-splotched face. I hitched my thumb back at the approaching car and told him here comes the money. Chuck refrained from comment. He just watched wordlessly as the car slid up beside mine and came to a short stop. The dust cloud engulfed us. Lenny Gay stepped out of the car coughing and sputtering and waving his hand in front of his face.

"Sorry for the lateness, Mr. Johnston," he said, still coughing. "My tennis ran a bit over this morning." He walked around the front of my car and we shook hands. In fact, he did look as if he had come directly from the country club, hanging a pair of European sunglasses from the front of his salmon colored golf shirt and smoothing out the road wrinkles in his pleated khaki shorts. He looked around through the settling dust, regarding the much less formally dressed Chuck with a passing nod. Chuck for his part watched Lenny as warily as if he had just stepped out of a flying saucer instead of an Audi.

"Ah," Lenny said, pointing up at the Cessna. "So this is it?"

I nodded yes.

"Have you chartered it yet?"

I opened my mouth to answer but Chuck cut me off at the pass.

"Whoa, whoa, whoa now," Chuck said. "Ain't nobody chartered nothing yet. You two're getting your horse and your cart flip-flopped. I ain't even said this here bird's up for charter yet."

Again I cleared my throat, which was beginning to get raw what with all the clearing and the dust. I reminded Chuck in as polite a tone as I could that what he *actually* said was that it depended.

"Depends on what exactly?" asked Lenny.

Money. Mostly.

"Of course," Lenny said. "Money, of course. How much money?"

Lenny looked at me. I looked at Chuck. Chuck sucked on his front teeth and looked back at Lenny.

"For the day," Chuck said. "Five thousand."

Lenny was quick on the draw. "Done."

"Plus fuel. You'd buy your own fuel."

"Very well." Lenny reached into his pocket and pulled out a leather-bound checkbook which he unfolded on the hood of my car. He clicked the pen. "Will a personal check do?"

Chuck was openly flummoxed. His mouth sagged as he looked greedily at the open checkbook. It was as if the man's mind was running a tally of what he could buy, all the pretty things he could buy. After a moment, he shook himself.

"Now hang on there," he said, regaining his senses. He drew himself up. "There's other things to consider here. Other than money, I mean."

Lenny straightened, unclicked the pen. "Such as?"

"Such as the weather."

Lenny put his hands on his hips impatiently. He looked up, his eyes slits against the blare of the sun. I shielded my own eyes and looked up into the sky. High white wisps of clouds that looked like cotton wads pulled thin sheeted the sky to the south and west but directly overhead was nothing but blue.

"Don't be ridiculous," said Lenny dismissively. "The weather couldn't possibly be more perfect."

"Right now that's true," agreed Chuck. "But this is springtime-turnin'-to-summer in Mis'Sippi, mister, and that means that what you see ain't always what you're gonna get."

I asked him if he'd seen something on the weather forecast.

"I don't waste my time on them weathermen. *So-called* weathermen. Bunch of good-for-nothings couldn't predict the temperature inside their own house much less out here. Naw, I listen to my knee and my knee says a storm's coming. And that makes it a probably. But unfortunately for you fellars, today my hip agrees and that makes it dern near a sure thing." He shook his head and spit out in front of him. He wiped his chin on his shoulder. "Couldn't let ya take her up in that. Not today."

Lenny clicked the pen again. He flashed the same off-center toothy grin that graced his Memphis-Metro bus-stop ads and television commercials. The ones with that cheesiest of cheesy jingle that incorporated his business's telephone number. The ones that had made him a familiar, if not exactly respected, household name in the Western Tennessee area. "Six thousand?"

This time it was Chuck's turn to respond quickly. "Done. You fill that check out, I'll gas her up. You got any cargo, mister?"

"Nope, just people," Lenny said bending back down to his checkbook. "One pilot and one passenger."

"Passenger?" I asked. "What passenger?"

He looked up at me smiling that ridiculous smile and that jingle from his ads recurred to me unbidden.

"You're looking at him," he said. "You didn't think I'd skip out on the third set of my doubles match, drive all the way out here, and put up six grand to let you take her up there all alone did you Mr. Johnston?" And he went back to filling out the check, the smile still on his face.

thirty-one

It still wasn't a done deal.

After Chuck had finished preparing the plane, he sauntered back over to us wiping his hands on a rag that had once been bright red but was now more grease splotched than any one particular color. He pinched Lenny's check with his thumb and forefinger near a corner as if the filth from his hands might invalidate it. He held it up close to his face and looked at it skeptically for quite a while.

"Hafta put a call in to your bank a'course," he said after his inspection of the check itself was complete.

"Of course," said Lenny.

As he walked back into the building, Chuck, or at least the bearer of Chuck's shirt, pointed around its far corner and spoke back over his shoulder, Lenny's check still pinched in his other hand.

"Coke machine's around back there," he said. "Price says fifteen cents but it's really a whole dollar. We ain't had it changed for inflation. But anyhow, just help yourself if your whistle needs wettin'. This might take a minute or two."

And so it had. As we sipped on our canned drinks in the shade of the clapboard shack, we heard Chuck verify the funds with nearly everyone at Lenny's bank, starting with the poor unfortunate teller that answered the phone all the way up the ladder to the branch manager. Finally we heard the phone hang up and we swigged down the last of our drinks. Chuck sauntered slowly around the desk and stood in the open doorway. He breathed out a long breath and measured me with another farmer-inspecting-his-crop look.

"Now you're the pilot?"

I said I was.

"Familiar with this sort of craft?"

Again, I was.

"Whatcha name?"

I told him.

"And what outfit did you say you fly for?"

I said that I *hadn't* said, not yet. And when he didn't laugh I told him Gulf Coastal.

Then he sucked his front teeth again and ran his tongue along the space between his lower lip and his gums. "Hafta put a call in on you, too, I reckon," he said. And before either of us had time to protest, he turned his back and disappeared back into the shack.

Twenty minutes later, he sauntered back out. By then it was seriously hot, the sun high overhead. Chuck set his cap back and wiped his forehead with the greasy rag. Then he poked the rag back into his hip pocket and didn't say anything for quite a while.

"And?" Lenny asked impatiently. "Do we have a deal or not?"

"'fraid not," he said. "It's a no-go."

Lenny looked at me in confusion, but I had foreseen this complication and was not shocked by it.

"What do you mean 'no-go'?" Lenny demanded.

"Well, your pilot here checked out with Gulf Coastal. Said he was a good enough flyer, no marks on his record or nothing."

"Well, that's good right?" Lenny looked towards me for support but I already knew where this was going. "Right?"

"But then the lady asked me if'n I wouldn't mind to pass a message along to you, Mr. Johnston, and I said of course I would, why not, and she said for me to tell you on the behalf of everybody down at Gulf Coastal that they's wishin' you a speedy recovery and I said oh was there something the matter and she said she should think so, said our Mr. Johnston here's been on disability for over six months due to injury. She said last her records say, he's paralyzed. Said he ain't been in the air since before Christmas, hell ain't *walked* since before Christmas. So I said thank ye kindly ma'am and hung up the phone and now I'm sayin' it's a no-go."

"Don't be absurd," spat Lenny. "All that's true, of course, but just look at him. He's certainly not paralyzed anymore. Even you can see that."

Chuck didn't take the insult.

"Don't matter," he said. "I've felt a storm comin' for two days now. I had a bad feeling in my gut when I saw you drive up, and now this." He spit and wiped his chin again. "If it was just the one thing then maybe, but it ain't just the one thing."

Lenny put his hands on his hips. I saw with amazement that he wasn't sweating, there wasn't even the fainted trace of moisture on his forehead. He stepped away from the building and pointed up at the Cessna, which stood motionless like a giant stuffed bird fifteen yards away. I imagined him surrounded by a courtroom, dressed in a fine three-piece suit instead of yacht clothes and I could see why he was good at what he does.

"That plane," he began, still pointing at the Cessna. It was his exhibit A. "You can't tell me you don't have it insured."

Chuck scoffed. "My momma didn't raise no dummy, if'n that's what you mean."

"No, of course she didn't."

Chuck gave as little indication of picking up on Lenny's sarcasm as he had the previous insult. I, on the other hand, had to fold my bottom lip back between my teeth to stifle the laughter that threatened to burst from me like the eruption of a massive volcano. Lenny continued.

"Allow me, if you will, to evaluate your situation. If it's a no-go as you say, you get no money plus you've wasted an entire morning on the telephone. And if I may repeat: you get no money, none. That's scenario number one. Scenario number two: you let us fly and we return unharmed, in which case you are six thousand dollars richer and six thousand dollars happier than you were when you woke up this morning. That's better."

Here was his closing argument. He stepped further back and rested his fingertips lightly on exhibits B and C; our cars, his on his right and mine on his left. Even in the direct rays of the sun, he was not sweating.

"But there's one more possibility. Say you let us fly and something bad *does* occur. Say your gut was right, or your knee was right, or my friend here suddenly loses function of his body again, or whatever. If that plane goes down, you'll get a hefty insurance pay-out, you'll still have the six grand, *and* you'll be holding the titles to two, count 'em, *two* automobiles, one of which, if I may say so myself is rather rare in these parts and rather fine. That's scenario number three."

Chuck looked at him thoughtfully, the hamster churning the wheel underneath his cap working hard.

"Now," Lenny concluded, "my friend and I are of course hoping for scenario number two. If I might take the liberty of speaking for Mr. Johnston, I don't think we would begrudge you for pulling for number three as it would leave you with the most compensation for your trouble, but either one involves us chartering that airplane. So what do you say, sir? Shall we tuck those car titles away in your office for safekeeping or would you rather us take our check and go?"

Chuck looked at Lenny, then he looked at me. He sucked his teeth, spit, and wiped. Finally his eyes settled on the Audi.

thirty-two

Ten minutes later, we sat in the cockpit of the Cessna, its engine vibrating beneath our feet. I went through the pre-flight checks while Lenny fumbled with the straps of the seatbelt.

"I took some flying lessons, you know."

I had been looking out at the left wing flaps, checking that their motion was free and unhindered. Satisfied, I paused briefly and glanced at Lenny who at last conquered the concept of the seatbelt and buckled in. But I didn't look for long, not wanting to see the white ceramic container he held crooked in one arm.

"Yep," he said, his voice coming through my headset clearly. "Right after law school. But I got partner very early and my free time went to zilch so I had to cut the classes. It's a shame, too. I had the feeling I would've made a good pilot."

I told him this should be a breeze then and I finished up my checks. Everything appeared to be in good shape. Better than good actually. Chuck, for all his other potential faults, took extremely good care of his airplane.

"Pre-flight a go?"

That was Chuck's voice in my ear.

I answered in the affirmative.

"You are a go for take-off. The strip is yours."

I copied that. And then I taxied the Cessna to the center of the runway, employing much the same technique as I had play-acted in my wheelchair with Miss Rosie's guidance. Memories of that day flipped before my eyes like a stack of polaroids and a spike of happiness pierced my heart. As I came to a full stop I realized I was smiling.

Just before I opened the throttle, I did look at the container cradled in Lenny's arm. I looked at it and thought not about its physical contents, but the life it represented. And I kept on smiling.

thirty-three

The engine swelled.

We started rolling, slowly at first but picking up steam. The engine swelled again, its hum rising from bass to baritone and now we were really moving. Every bump in the strip was a jostle in the cockpit. The blue above us never changed but the green began to blur along our periphery. I could feel the speed, feel the pressure sucking me into the pilot's seat. But at the same time, I could feel the lightness of it, like I could simply jump and float away. Like what-goes-up-must-come-down was a truth for everyone else but not for me, not here in this plane, not with these wings out beside me and my hands on the controls.

That baritone was rising, every mechanical part below our feet spinning and pumping and gearing so smoothly I forgot they were there. The throttle opened all the way up and then even the baritone hum melted away. The strip with all its tiny imperfections melted away. The rolling canvas of green on our either side melted away. Everything melted away. There was the sky and there was me. I pulled back and we became lighter than air and the earth began to fall away. I picked us up over the green hands of the trees and we kept on climbing. Up, up, up. I had jumped and now I was floating away.

thirty-four

Lenny's face was a bloodless white.

"Are you going to be okay?" I asked through my microphone.

Lenny looked around, startled, his eyes just as much whites as they were irises. His blueish lips looked unnatural as they formed words like a badly painted mannequin. "Wh-who? Me?"

Of course, I had wanted to say something smart. Something like, "No, no, not *you* Lenny. I was just asking one of our *other* passengers if *they* were alright." But then a little angel popped up on my shoulder and reminded me of Miss Rosie's letter and how she had said for me to be kind to Lenny Gay. So the miniature devil on my other shoulder vanished with a poof.

"Yes, Lenny." I said patiently. "You look a little pale. Are you going to be alright?"

"Oh, do I?" He passed a hand over his face and giggled nervously. His hand came away wet with sweat and I thought about how he hadn't sweated a drop during his negotiations with Chuck. And that was after about an hour out in the heat. His eyes bugged out the window, looking down and he giggled again. "You must think me a lightweight, Mr. Johnston. It's just that I've never flown in anything this small before. It makes falling seem like a more likely thing. Just do me a favor and don't do any barrel-rolls or loop-de-loops or anything."

Again, he giggled but I could see he wasn't joking. If I tried anything, he would lose his breakfast. What I needed to do was get his mind off the ground and the best way to do that was to get his eyes away from the window.

"Tell you what," I said, reaching behind my seat and searching with my hand. "I don't exactly know where I'm headed and if I'm going to do this job correctly, I'm going to need a navigator. You up for it?" Then my hand found what it was searching for and I handed a stack of folded paper to Lenny. It was Miss Rosie's grandfather's map. Gene had gotten it from his new shed's attic for me. It still carried a musty trunk smell within its folds.

"Navigator?" Lenny asked taking the map. His face was already pinking up. "I could do that, yeah."

He unfolded the map and started scanning it with a finger.

"Okay, Leonard," he mumbled to himself, but with his voice coming through my headset all the same. "Where are you?"

"The airstrip we just took off from should be highlighted in yellow. And we're headed south and west."

Lenny's finger found the highlighted rectangle and then traced a straight line down and to his left. "Ah-ha," he said delighted. "Then we should be coming up on Fox Bottom Creek."

At that very moment, I spotted the signature break in the trees that indicates a ravine or a river and as we flew closer, I saw a brown ribbon of flowing creek water. I dipped our right wing and pointed, announced, "Fox Bottom Creek." Lenny spared a glance out his window and immediately his face turned a shade of green reserved for animated frogs and other such amphibians.

"Sorry," I said. "Forgot."

Lenny held a finger up to hush me as the lump in his throat traveled up and then down again in a slow conscious swallow, keeping his Eggs Benedict and cranberry juice from coming up, no doubt. I brought the plane back to level and Lenny turned his miscolored face back to the map. He pointed to his right without looking up.

"A little more that way, I think," he said. "Gently though. Gently."

I turned us a bit more west.

"Like that?"

Lenny looked at the map.

"Exactly," he said. "It should be a straight shot. Just keep heading directly..."

His voice trailed off as his head came up. I looked over and saw that his jaw was loose and his mouth was hanging open. Then I looked forward and saw what he was seeing. Those high wispy clouds we had observed from the Littleton Airstrip had coalesced and darkened into a thick rolling wave. As we watched, bubbles of lightning exploded from somewhere within it. The closer we got, the darker and more foreboding it appeared. It was if someone had pulled the drapes over the brightness of the day.

Chuck's knee had been right. His hip had been even righter. A storm, it was acomin'.

"Relax," I told Lenny. "Those clouds are still a good distance away and we'll be on the ground in just a few more minutes." I opened the throttle up and our airspeed increased. But already I could feel the occasional gust of wind pound against the Cessna like a mighty invisible fist. An impossibly bright bolt of lightning shot down from the center of the blackness and struck the earth. As I blinked away the afterimage, I looked over and saw that Lenny's eyes were pinched closed and he was whimpering, his mouth quivering wordlessly.

"The first time I visited Miss Rosie it came a storm like this," I said.

Lenny's mouth stopped moving. He was listening and that was good.

"She had just asked me to tell her a story about the first time I went flying. But before I could even begin, lightning struck a tree in her backyard. In all the time I knew her, I never got to tell her that story."

thirty-five

I was young, only nineteen.

The instructor was sipping black coffee in the seat beside me. He was a real salty dog, this instructor, being the only son of a fisherman and having flown numerous missions from aircraft carriers during the conflict in Vietnam. The rumor on him was that nothing could get him flustered, having survived the war and then weathering numerous hurricanes, botched tattoos, and ugly divorces. My best friend back then, Paul Glassier used to joke that he was living proof that the Navy amputated their pilots' adrenal glands during wartimes to keep them calm under pressure.

"How 'bout a barrel roll?"

I ventured a laugh and glanced over at the Salty Dog, expecting some indication that he was joking. His skin was leathery tan except for where it was tattoo green and his beard was bleached white everywhere but for the nicotine stains around his mouth. He gulped down the last of his coffee and set the mug underneath his seat. But he did not smile.

I asked him if he was serious. Did he know this was my first time at the controls? Barrel roll? I've logged maybe fifteen minutes airtime and he wants me to do a barrel roll?

"You gotta learn sometime, don't you?" he said, his voice a bear's growl. "Might as well give it a shot now. And besides, it ain't too tough a move. We'll only be upside-down for a second or two."

And so he told me what to do. The key, he said, was to hold the turn, all the way through, no matter what. He said that natural tendency was to slack off the controls when you're flipped belly-up. That the human brain is convinced that half a roll is somehow good enough.

"That'll kill you quicker'n a hick-up," he said.

I nodded, my headset bouncing up and down.

"Now, repeat it back to me."

And so I did, including the part about dying faster than a diaphragm spasm.

"Good," he said. "Now just do it."

I licked my dry lips with my dry tongue and looked out my window. We were over a long stretch of Florida swamplands, the gleam of the sun reflecting up through thin patches of grass and the occasional collection of shrubby trees. I looked out ahead and tried to imagine the spot we would go down, wondering if we would explode on impact or drown upside-down as the plane sunk deeper and deeper into the swamp.

"Go on," growled the Salty Dog. "I'm only getting older and more ornery."

I looked at him with eyes that must have been swimming with fright and asked him for the last time if he was sure about this. I mean *absolutely positively* sure. His reply was a flat expressionless stare.

So I took a massive deep breath and sent up a quick selfish prayer of survival and spun the controls like I thought they should be spun. The sky and the ground swapped places. The shrubs hung down like green bristly stalactites. Clouds lay here and there like pillows strewn across a big blue carpet. The sun shone up and its swampy reflection shone down. And from somewhere far off in a distant world, an alarm was sounding.

I only realized that my hands were off the controls when we flipped back over and my arms flopped back down to my side. They had been dangling on either side of my head as I stared dreamily at the upside-down world I had created. Somehow, the alarm had stopped. With a start, I grabbed the yoke with both hands only to realize that it had a life of its own, moving subtly forward and back and left and right, keeping us level.

"Take a breather," said the Salty Dog, his cowhide hands on his own set of controls. "I've got it for a while."

We flew along silently for what felt like hours. During that time, I tried diligently to find interesting scenery outside my window. I preoccupied myself with pulling a stubborn piece of hangnail or smoothing out my shirt or, when that was taken care of, looking back out my window at the monotonous stretch of nothingness. Finally, I felt the plane dip a bit as my instructor let go of the controls.

"Time to give it another go."

I grabbed my version of the yoke and did what I'd been avoiding since I almost converted this lesson into a local news blurb involving two fatalities. I looked at him.

"Go on," he grunted. He drew a circle in the air with one cigarette-yellowed fingertip. "Again."

The wideness of my eyes and the wordless gape of my mouth was asking if he could possibly be serious. Another barrel-roll? Another hick-up close brush with death?

"You panicked," he said. No expression, no anger, no compassion, no nothing on his face. "You knew what to do and you didn't do it. You let go. You did nothing when just doing something, *anything* would have been better. You panicked and you let go. Now, once is a mistake, twice is a habit, and more than that is just who you are. So try it again."

And so I did.

thirty-six

We touched down just as the worst of rain began to fall. It was going to be a soaker; fat drops of water pelted the fuselage and wings of the Cessna, roaring the interior of the cockpit, but it was also going to be an abbreviated affair. Already, there brimmed a blue line above the treetops that held promise for a speedy end to the storm.

I pointed past the black clouds towards that blueness and told Lenny that we could wait it out, that it shouldn't last long. He nodded and sat with his arms folded over his chest, seemingly content to be reunited with the earth. I patched Chuck in on the radio and relayed our whereabouts, assuring him that we were both alive and that his precious aircraft was uninjured. He gave a standard callback, concealing his relief or possible disappointment and giving no indication whether or not he was inspecting the additional luxury features of Lenny's car.

We sat awkwardly there for some time, not talking, just listening to the roar of the cockpit and watching the water cascade down the windshield. For myself, I was trying not to think, trying to turn my mind off, but failing. The harder I tried, the harder I failed. As for Lenny, I'll never know for sure, but I imagine it was the same for him. There is no avoiding some measure of deep reminiscing when laying to rest the remains of a friend, be it during a graveside service or what we were about to do, and I believe we were both indulging in that subconscious look back over our experiences with Miss Rosie Cotcher as that storm passed directly over the old R. and C. Cotcher Airstrip heading northeast toward Chuck and his weathervane hip and knee.

And then, without a word from either of us, the rain slacked and died, the sky blued, and the heat, although not quite as viscous as before, returned.

We unbuckled and got out of the Cessna, our feet landing on rain-softened earth. I looked around. Although the area had grown up, it had not been completely grown over. Tall grass that could easily be cut, raked, and bailed into hay swayed green and golden in the light easterly breeze, but the age-old strip was still visible, a straight line of shorter field grass spotted with dandelions and onion-tufts running from where I stood nearly to the treeline. A kudzo-crawled structure stood about twenty yards from my end of the strip, the door missing, the windows busted out, the roof caved in.

The sound of a pulpwood truck snapped me around. I circled the Cessna, squishing in puddles which were already beginning to evaporate, and I noticed the highway ran just on the other side of a thin stand of ditch brush, baby blackjacks and pines mostly. Traffic heading back and forth between Millwood Branch and Martin could be glimpsed through the scrub and seen fully at the access point which was built up with a culvert and barred by a chain with pieces of bright orange plastic dangling from it.

Lenny looked from the chain to me. "Are we trespassing, Mr. Johnston?"

I smiled with a face that must have somewhat resembled the old me and told him that one was only trespassing if one was *caught* trespassing and that even if one *was* caught trespassing, who better to litigate one's way out of such charges than Leonard Buford Gay.

"So you're saying what?" he asked, picking up on my meaning. "We should hurry?"

I told him that's exactly what I was saying. He nodded and ducked back into the plane, reemerging with the ceramic container held carefully in both hands. Then he held it out, offering it to me.

"It should be you," he said. "although it's not technically part of your requirement. Miss Rosie said you promised her you two would fly again and now that you have, the legal part is over. But between the two of us, you knew her better and longer and so I just think it would be right if it were you that did the, you know..."

He gestured tipping the container, although he pressed one hand firmly down on the lid and was careful not to tip it too far. I agreed and took the canister from Lenny, using two hands as he had done although it was no more heavy than a can of coffee grounds. For a while, we just stood there, waiting for nothing other than the right moment. And then, as if by way of a signal, the birds took up a carefree call and response from their perches high in the trees. The sun was high, the air held a clean scent of Mother Earth after a shower, the breeze was combing the grass in gentle back and forths, and just as I was about to remove the lid and send Miss Rosie on her way, a car pulled from the highway and nosed onto the access drive. It stopped just shy of the barricading chain.

"Should we run?"

I responded to Lenny by ruefully pointing out that I was no Bo Duke and our chartered Cessna was no General Lee. By the time we got saddled back up and ready to take the air, whoever it was in that car would have time to call the sheriff and have us arrested three times over. And besides, I knew that car, knew it about as well as I knew my own KIA, and unless my ex-wife had made a recent land purchase in Hickahala County, I didn't think a hasty get-away would be necessary.

So we watched as the car door swung open and Tiffany Johnston popped out. She stepped delicately around her car and the metal post that held up one end of the chain and then made her way through the lower half of the field to where we stood in front of the Cessna.

"I don't mean to interrupt," she said, walking in an exaggerated semicircle to dodge a large patch of mud. "I would have been here on time, but-" She looked around a bit nervously, her eyes lighting upon Miss Rosie's canister and flitting away. "She told me the where but even she didn't know the when."

I made quick introductions and Tiffany shook Lenny's hand.

"So when exactly did Miss Rosie tell you about all this?" Lenny asked, barely concealing his confusion.

"About a week ago. When it looked like a good bet that Eric would be leaving the hospital soon. I thought it was a little morbid, to invite someone you barely knew to something that, at least in my mind, should be so private, but she insisted."

I asked her why she didn't just tell me, why the secrecy.

"I assumed Miss Rosie had it all worked out with you," she said. "As for me, I've been trying to call you for the past two days but your phone is completely dead. I had to contact Mr. Gay's office just to find out when you were coming out here. Thanks to those commercials I didn't even have to look up the number. Anyway, with the drive and all, I honestly thought I would miss the whole thing."

I looked at Lenny and he looked at me. Those looks said a lot. They corroborated that indeed neither of us had invited Tiffany. They said to leave it to Miss Rosie to manipulate the situation even after her earthly body was reduced to ashes. They also said that although we weren't expecting the unexpected, we weren't surprised by the surprise. We knew Miss Rosie better than that.

"No worries," said Lenny. "You're just in time. Mr. Johnston, I suggest we carry on. Before anyone else arrives."

I looked at them both and nodded. Then I wished Miss Rosie Godspeed and did what we came for.

thirty-seven

The take-off was smooth, then silence set in.

Lenny had insisted on driving Tiffany's car back to the Little-ton-Carr County Airstrip citing an evidently weak stomach and sudden aversion to flying. Furthermore, he insisted that Tiffany take his seat on the Cessna citing my need for a navigator and his need to get his money's worth for the charter. Lenny, of course, presented a good argument and Tiffany, of course, agreed.

"How is Megan?"

It was the only thing I could think of to break the silence channeling into my headset.

"She's good. With the Freemans. I would have brought her along, but..."

She hesitated. I tried to help her.

"You don't owe me an explanation," I said. "Believe it or not, I'd understand if you never let me see her again."

"No, it's not you, Eric. It's just that she really liked Miss Rosie and I didn't want to break her little heart."

I cleared my throat, checked the throttle, banked us a degree or two to the left.

"I think that was a good decision."

"Really?"

"Of course it was. Don't get me wrong, I would have loved to have seen her jump out of that car with you, but you had her best interests at heart and as long as that's the case, as far as I'm concerned, every decision you make is a good one."

She looked at me. I could feel her eyes but I didn't look over.

"You're a good mother, Tiff," I continued. "You've done a great job with our little girl. A much better job than I would have done."

Outside our headsets, the plane hummed. At last, she opened her mouth to speak but I cut her off.

"One last thing and I'll shut-up."

She closed her mouth and I could almost hear her listening, like the buzz of a disconnected telephone receiver or the sounds of the surf in an empty seashell.

"I'm sorry. For what I did. I haven't said it, I guess because I didn't know how, but I'm saying it now, the best I can. I'm very, very sorry."

Except for when I cleared our landing with Chuck, neither of us spoke for the rest of the flight.

thirty-eight

   This, I assume, is where I should tie off loose ends and taper
my story to its end.
   Over the next few weeks, I worked at setting my life back
right-side-up, beginning, at Tiffany's behest, with reconnecting
my phone. Next, I went to Shop-Rite and stocked up on groceries
as most of the contents of my refrigerator and pantry had long
since expired. I verified the balance of my account at the bank, en-
during a prolonged stare from the twenty-something teller who
no doubt had heard a number of rumors regarding my extended
absence involving anything up to and including my death. After
that, it became abundantly clear that although Miss Rosie had
made provisions for the payment of my medical debts, the Eric
Johnston coffers were by no means overflowing. Therefore, after
clearing a required series of occupational and physical tests, I returned to work with Gulf Coastal with a normal slate of flights.
   Things between Tiffany and myself improved to the point that
she allowed me to see Megan again, but it was a gradual process.
At first, I could only visit her at the East Memphis house. Just for
an hour or so, just long enough for a cup of imaginary tea and a
couple of imaginary biscuits buttered with an imaginary spread.
If it was late, she would let me read Megan a story and tuck her in.
Then after a few such visits, Tiffany drove out to Millwood Branch

and we all went for ice cream at the Dairy Bar and then sat at the ball fields and watched the little league games. I showed them around town and gave them the grand tour of the Bakers' house, which I had of course straightened and cleaned and scrubbed laboriously earlier that day.

From that night on, I had Megan every other weekend.

Then, everything seemed to settle into a comfortable place. I flew during the week. I attended church on Sundays, sitting in the front pew now. I got to know my daughter and she got to know me. I got to buy her toys and books and cookies and pies. We got to watch big things like the fireworks display at the town's Freedom Festival and little things like the Wilbanks twins's attempts to patch the potholes in Main Street outside my front window. And best of all, I got to watch her grow up, bit by bit, inch by inch.

My story, a chapter of it at least, seemed to have found its happiest ending.

But Miss Rosie, as I came to find out, wasn't quite finished with me.

thirty-nine

It was a Sunday, one of my Sundays with Megan.

We sat side-by-side on the front pew through the morning service, Megan doodling in her Noah and the Ark coloring book, myself following along with Gene's sermon in my leather-bound Bible. The message that Sunday was a good one, one for which even Miss Rosie might not threaten to move her membership. Gene, although even he might not have been consciously aware of it, preached it in the same genuine voice with which he had spoken to me the day I showed him around Miss Rosie's grounds. It was on the subject of our overwhelming capacity to sin, to stumble, to make a total mess of things and God's overwhelming capacity for grace. It was on achieving the ofttimes formidable task of forgiving, not only others, but ourselves. Especially ourselves. In short, it was about moving on.

About halfway through, Megan closed her coloring book and slid her green crayon back into its box and stacked them beside her on the pew. From the corner of my eye, I watched with what could only be fatherly pride as she adjusted them until they were just so. Then she laid her head over on my lap and fell asleep. I didn't stir her until Gene made the Invitation and the congregation rose for the final hymn.

It was *Amazing Grace, How Sweet the Sound* and we sang each verse.

Once it was sung and the dismissal prayer prayed, I gathered up my Bible and Megan's coloring book and crayons in one hand and took her little hand in my other and turned toward the front doors. I had planned on shaking a few hands on my way out, then taking my daughter to town for a bite of lunch but there, blocking my path, was Nora Jo, four months pregnant and just beginning to show.

"Mr. Johnston," she said with urgency, "come with me. There is someone you just have to meet. You too, little Megan, you too."

Then she grabbed me under the arm like she's used to doing and led me down the middle aisle. Poor Megan had to run to keep up until finally, I reached down and picked her up in my free arm. I nodded apologetically to the folks we bumped past but there was no slowing down Nora Jo and there was no escaping her grip. We zoomed past Gene, who was shaking hands in the foyer, with little more than a passing notation that it was an enjoyable sermon from me and suddenly, we were outside in the sunshine.

And from here, you know the rest.

Nora Jo brought us straight to where she had made you promise to wait for us. She introduced me and I introduced Megan. My first thought, other than how beautiful you were, of course, was that I didn't realize there were any more Cotchers living in this area. If I remember correctly, I believe I said as much. You opened your mouth and Nora Jo characteristically cut in edgewise.

"Oh Ms. Cotcher's not from these local parts, Mr. Johnston," she said. "In fact, she's not even from a *neighboring state*." This she said as if being from anywhere other than the Hospitality State itself, Arkansas, Alabama, Tennessee, or, Heaven-forbid, Louisiana was on par with being from a colony on the surface of the Moon. She went on to explain that you had just recently flown in from Austin, adding that, ding-ding-ding, Austin was a city way out in Texas, as if I hadn't known. You were here to collect family heirlooms, pictures and such, from Miss Rosie's stash in her shed. She had tracked you down before she had died and sent word insisting that someone from Carl Cotcher's side of the family take possession of what she called "the irreplacables" because she was the last of what remained of Rufus's side and she would be gone soon.

At some point, Nora Jo melted away the way the earth melts away just before take-off and in the span of a breath, there was only me and you.

I asked if you liked caramel pie. Remember? I asked if you liked caramel pie and I wasn't going to let Nora Jo answer for you on that one. Megan and I were just about to have lunch at the Dairy Bar and we had plans to follow it up with a slice or two. It might be the kind of place that sticks your receipt in your french fry plate, the Dairy Bar, but they made a pretty good caramel pie. Very good actually. Especially when Fannie's the one working the kitchen, which I had by a reliable source she was this very afternoon.

But I was rambling.

I apologized.

Did you say you liked it?

Caramel pie?

"Caramel pie?" you asked. "Why, I guess I'd be a fool not to."

The Traveler

He had the girls in stitches so I came out front to see why the fuss. Why work wasn't being done. They were all in such riotous laughter they never heard me. He was still working on his shirttails. His left arm from the elbow down didn't work well, hadn't since Mr. Truman had sent him to Korea, and despite my best efforts, simple things like buttoning up and tucking in were no longer simple.

I cleared my throat and the girls jumped to. I must have appeared quite foreboding in my long white coat, much like an undertaker's but opposite in color. The younger ones blushed but ole Bet never hitched up. Intimidation and other such trivialities were worn-out useless tactics with Bet. She'd known me too long.

"My, Mr. Mac," she said without a second glance in my direction. "I never knew you had been to so many places."

"Ayuh," he said. "I been all over. All over the world really."

Bet loved to get folks talking, especially those long in the tooth. She fed on it.

"Tell an old girl about Paris, would you Mr. Mac?"

So he did. As he shamelessly stuffed his corduroys full of starch-ironed shirttails with his good hand, he laid out Paris. The younger bunch batted their lashes and breathed the word back, but not ole Bet. She just sat and listened, soaking it all in.

He finished with, "It's not all in the brick and mortar, that town. Most of what it is you gotta feel. You gotta *breathe*." And they sighed again, the sounds of never-hads and never-wills.

He was buttoning his cuffs with slow determination. Ole Bet kept on and he was more than willing to oblige her.

Rome was an old place. It felt important but more than that, it felt old.

The Swiss were a beautiful people.

Africa had been hot. But not at all like he expected.

He had forgotten and left his grandaddy's Bible on the bed in a Tokyo hotel room. It had only been a three day trip and he had lost his grandaddy's Bible.

By the time he had wrestled on his jacket, we had gone half-way around the world. His hat was curled in his hand and I felt a lull. I spoke into it.

"Where's the best place, Mr. Mac?"

He pulled his hat on, used both hands to straighten it as best he could. A twinkle lit his eyes and he shot a wink over at Bet.

"Son," he said, "I'll put it this a-way. I don't live in France or Switzerland or anyplace else."

He turned and held the door open for my ten-thirty. With a final tip of the hat, he was gone. The girls all got quiet and still. Then, as one, they started pushing their pens and shuffling their papers and answering their phones.

I drifted through the remainder of the morning. I daydreamed through my turkey on rye at Dixie's and then kept on drifting. At quarter of five, I checked out. I didn't even consider the stir-fry in my freezer or the unopened bottle in the fridge. I just pointed it toward Muddy Pine Ridge and drove until I was there.

I was just in time. I got out and walked until my car was a well-forgotten thing. I sat in the cattail and listened as the breeze gave them song. I worked the air in and out of my lungs. I dug my fingers into the soil. I watched the sun lay itself into sheets of purple satin and thought about the best place.

A Sunset for a Suicidist

Belle dug her fingers into the sand and cupped out a sugar white handful and lifted it to eye level. Tiny avalanches slid down the sides of her mini-mountain. Fine trickles through the cracks between her fingers. She cupped her hand tighter, felt the particles compact, rub past one another, grit together and apart again. The more she gripped, the more she lost until at last there was nothing but a single layer of glistening grains clinging to the spaces between the creases of her palm. Then she drew her hand across the thigh of her shorts and there was nothing at all.

The knife had been a wedding gift. A set of knives actually. Plastic, cheap little things. A rooster in relief on the white handle. A rooster of all things. They had come from someone on Phil's side, of course, and Belle's first thought after opening them up and putting on a smile was that they would never no-not-ever go anywhere near her kitchen. She was marrying Phil Carroll, the self-made insurance juggernaut of the Mid-South, for goodness sakes and one of his hick relatives thought she would use a set of rooster knives from Po-dunk Dry Goods and General Store?

But she had. They both had. And who could blame them? The blades were sharp, as sharp as the two-hundred dollar set of

Schlitzers she had bought at Duphrane's, and a million times handier. They didn't require sharpening or hand-washing or storage in a foam-lined cedar box. They were there and they could handle the job and so they used them. The rooster knives, like so many other bits of hum-drum, had slivered their way into the routine of her life.

But all that would be over soon.

The sun kissed the water somewhere beyond the horizon and lit a trail of red that terminated in the froth churned up by the crashing waves directly in front of her. The waves themselves lapped up and were swept back, lapped up and swept back, each one leapfrogging the one before as the tide pulled the ocean closer and closer to where her toes had unconsciously dug themselves into the cool Emerald Coast sand.

Soon. At sunset. A matter of mere minutes.

The wedding had been beautiful, of course. Belle had seen to that herself. A six o'clock wedding with lit candles and roses of the deepest red. All the while she had made momentary comparisons to the wedding in her mind, the one she had visualized as far back as she could remember, and at every juncture, she had made a mental check mark. The roses and the candles were a must and the first two checks. The bridesmaids' dresses - check. The *Ave Maria*. The vows. The veil. The kiss. And at the reception, the lily white chair covers tied on with silk ribbons and set off with a single lone rose at the back. Check, check, and check.

Nothing, even in the slightest of degrees, went wrong. It was as if the wedding in her mind had been played out before her like a well blocked play. That night, after Phil had rolled over to his side of the bed and tucked his arm under his pillow the way that even then she had known would become his nightly staple, she had felt emptied out. Her fantasy, jettisoned into the void of reality. And in the hollow place it had occupied, a collection of check marks, as worthless as a sack of gravel. She hadn't dreamed that night and she had awoken to the fear that her days of dreaming were coming to an end.

The sun, she watched as it dipped further into the ocean, half in and half out. Its skirts spread at the bottom into a shimmery gathering of pink and purple lace. The air was warm, but the source of the heat reached out to her sideways, across the buffering of the water and the waves and the sand. Belle drank in the air as the sun drank in the ocean. Sinking, ever sinking, speeding away to the other side of the world.

Phil's business was already well established when Belle tethered herself to his hitch, but it was nothing compared to the kingdom it had become in these last few years. He had been popular growing up; quarterback and place-kicker on the high school football team and who could ever forget that one-hit shutout he pitched in the state championship series? So, as a young unmarried, selling life insurance policies and forbearances among his friends' parents and, in some rare occasions, grandparents had been enough for him to strike out on his own but not enough for much more. That changed, however, as he aged. Insurance, he would say, comes better from someone with a little gray in his hair. And he was right; his clientship increased with each candle added to his cake.

Then came Belle and the wedding plucked directly from her imagination like a petal from a rose. Word spread that Phil, yes Phil Carroll the Insurance Man down in Littleton, was married, that he understood the complexities of ensuring a spouse's well-being after the other is gone. And of course there was the billboard, the one with his smiling mug on one side, ten feet tall, slightly receding hairline and hint of white sweeping in at the temples, parentheses framing his grin. Phil Carroll Cares it said in gold-hued block letters next to the picture. It had been his snake on a staff, that billboard. And they had flocked to him like some sort of messiah, the kind that promised not life, but a check for your surviving beneficiaries if your death occurs in the proper manner and within the proper timeframe.

Business boomed when he put up that billboard. That had been shortly after their fourth anniversary. Then came the twins and it absolutely exploded.

The water had reached her feet, pooling in the little trenches made by the soft curve of her heels, swirling in minuscule eddies each time a wave came and went. The dying light of the day painted the water a red that once again reminded Belle of her wedding ceremony, the roses and the candlelight. She picked up the rooster knife and noted that the blade, sharper than any in the high-dollar set she had bought at Duphrane's, threw back the same red light. A big wave crested and crashed and drowned her feet up to her ankles. The sun was but an orange peel peeking over the tabletop of the sea.

Belle had gotten pregnant right on schedule. Five years into the marriage, to the week, and she experienced a sudden and un-questionable aversion to her morning grapefruit half. One morn-ing it was fine as ever - she had split a fresh one, place one half in a bowl, sprinkled on her no-calorie sweetener and dug in, the other she wrapped in aluminum and placed in the fridge - and the next, the mere thought of her spoon stabbing into the pulpy fruit made her tongue swell with pre-vomit hypersalivation. She had slammed the refrigerator door with the aluminum-covered semi-sphere still inside and kissed Phil on the cheek and shooed him off to the office and waited ten minutes. Ten anxiety-ridden minutes. She had forced herself to sit and placed her right hand over her pitter-pattering heart as if she were pledging allegiance. Then she had found her biggest pair of sunglasses and pulled her ponytail through the back of one of Phil's caps and scampered into her Viper and drove to the pharmacy all the way down in Martin.

Although there was no denying the double pink lines that ap-peared on the dipstick in the restroom of the drug store, she took the test again as soon as she got home and then one final time the following morning while Phil was on the treadmill. When the results were the same, she made another mental check mark and, despite the babies growing in her belly, felt even more empty inside. Like she had lost another chunk of that precious secret life she had nurtured since she was a tiny girl.

The boys had just turned one when she found the website. Tips for the Successful Suicidist, it had been called. Its existence confirmed, at least to Belle, that you could find anything on the internet. The site was small, only one page, but she waited until Phil was at work and the boys were down for their mid-morning nap before she revisited it on their MacBook and read it fully.

Step 1: Make a plan.

Step 2: Stick to your plan.

Step 3: Do not write a note. If you feel compelled to write a note, you do not really want to do this.

Step 4: Do not say goodbye. It will only change your mind. --- See Step 2.

Step 5: Do not use a firearm. Too many things beyond your control could potentially go wrong. You will just have to trust us on this one.

Step 6: Do not drink. Intoxication increases the likelihood of a botch. In addition, if you feel compelled to drink, you do not really want to do this.

Step 7: Take your time. Think about it. Once you decide, however you decide, commit yourself totally.

That had been six months ago. In the meantime, Phil had gotten balder, richer, and more ingratiated in the boys' eyes. They were becoming Carrolls, both of them, right before her eyes. Phil was teaching them to throw, showing them how to cock their arms behind their heads and Let-Her-Rip-Just-Like-The-Old-Man. It would only be a matter of sixteen or so years before they had the family crest, which was simply the word Carroll in gothic lettering, tattooed across their shoulders, too.

A matter of time.

Time. And that's all.

And then that chunk of her little life would be lost with the rest of it. Into the Black Land of the Check Marks. Gone forever, no matter how hard she gripped.

So she had packed the rooster knife in the zipper pouch of her bathroom bag. For extra measure, she had wrapped it in a silk shoulder wrap she hadn't worn since she was pregnant. She had unzipped the pouch and peered inside at least twenty times throughout her packing process to ensure that all that could be seen were the soft folds of sunflower-print fabric. No blade, no rooster. If someone dug their hand down inside that pouch to feel around, she would have some rather uncomfortable questions to answer but Belle was confident that wouldn't happen. She was a meticulous packer and if Phil ever needed something, say a new spool of dental floss or say the brown belt that he only wore on the rare occasions he allowed himself to wear jeans, something that he didn't already know the location of, he would typically ask her to point it out straightaway before rummaging around.

It had been in the back of her mind the entire drive down, that rooster knife. She had spun to check on the boys in the second seat of the Suburban more than the usual amount and each time, her eyes flicked to the rear-most compartment of the vehicle, the compartment that held their luggage and the wedding gift about which only she had known. It had ridden down to Florida with them the way a dirty country bumpkin, bare-chested and black-teethed, might ride stowaway-style between the cars of a fancy passenger train.

They had arrived at the condo at half past nine and she had put the twins straight to bed as Phil unloaded the luggage. Jonathan rubbed his night-night blankey across his cheek and fell straight to sleep just as if they were at home but Joel was fidgety and she was forced to soothe away his nervous energy by lightly scratching his back and singing that song about Aunt Nancy and her ill-fated gray goose until at last he slumped bonelessly in her arms. All the while, she had half-expected Phil to enter the boys' temporary bedroom holding the little rooster knife with her shoulder wrap draped down from it like the peel from a banana and ask her what the devil was *this* doing in the pouch she usually kept her tampons in.

But of course, that didn't happen. She'd tucked Joel in and set a light-lipped kiss on Jonathan's eyebrow and backed slowly out of the room humming ever softer verses of that odd and tragic lullaby. As she crossed over the threshold, the tune receded totally, leaving a silence in her throat that felt final and irretrievable, as if some great and wonderful thing had just slipped from her fingers and fallen down a well. She turned then and stood in the doorway of their own bedroom, Phil propped up on a pillow-laden headboard and the covers on her side dog-eared. The latest issue of her favorite gossip magazine was laid by on the nightstand with her readers on top, its half-moon lenses holding lamplight like two tiny beacons. And in her mind, a check mark, so thick and bold it eclipsed all doubt.

The next day, she awoke before Phil and the boys as per usual. She poured her coffee and slipped out onto the patio and listened to the distant waves as the sun crept purposefully up over the condo-tops. She decided there, with her mug perched just below her lower lip, her breath cooling its dark surface, that her original plan was as sound as it was simple.

Phil wasn't a drunkard, but he did possess a certain enjoyment for drinking beer on the beach. At times during previous trips to the coast, he would drink can after can until Belle made a subtle suggestion he stop. Today, she would make no such suggestion.

You work hard all year, she would say.

This is your vacation, she would say.

You do as you please, she would say.

And then she would dip into the cooler and fetch him another.

The twins would be even easier. She would skimp on their midmorning and afternoon naps and that, in combination with the draining potential of the sun and vigorous bouts of playtime either on the beach itself or at the condo's kiddie pool, should set them up for a nice long evening nap.

And while they slept, Phil with a bellyful of imported beer and the boys with headfuls of whatever little boys dream about when they are happy and carefree and exhausted, she would slip back out to the beach with her handy little knife and watch as the sun went down.

The plan, of course, went off without a hitch. Check, check, check, just as everything always had in her little life. Check, check, check. A perfect sort of misery of which she could never tell anyone without seeming anything other than spoiled rotten. Not her friends in the auxiliary, not her doctor, and chief of all, not Phil Carroll, a man built to view life and death with statistician eyes.

Palaces can be prisons, and princesses may never complain.

She hadn't said goodbye. She hadn't left a note. She hadn't drank a drop.

As the sun threw its final spears of red light across the water, she lay back. Her dark hair haloed around her head. The sand, a bed. The waves, a lullaby.

She closed her eyes and thought of roses.

What the Storm Did

It was early when we got there. The sun was no more than a gray vagueness laying low against what remained of the treetops. A drizzle hung in the air, swirling into a fine mist when it came to the old rooster wind-chime, the corners of the house, the bill of my cap. Although my t-shirt was soon thickened by its moisture, it was but an anticlimax compared to the downpour of the night before. In the backyard, our boots sucked and sloshed in the mud and we skated more than walked down the hill. We nodded to those already there but the only sounds were the slaps and patters of drips into the flat hands of leaves and we left it that a-way.

At the bottom of the hill lay a bare patch of Earth, almost a perfect square. Cement blocks stacked in the corners, three high. The tin shed that had been stilted on those blocks for decades had been tossed onto its roof twenty yards away. Looking at it, I remembered fetching a countless number of cartons of peas or beans or creamed corn on nights long-lost. A child's errand for his grandmother. It had seemed so indefinite, that shed, so permanently a part of the landscape. Like the clay-wash on the other side of the road or the three strands of barbed wire pulled tight along the north line of the orchard. Now it was a mangle of scrap metal in a place it didn't belong.

A couple of us wormed our way inside. Glass shards from broken pickle jars lay in clusters here and there. A bent pair of crutches. Opaque garbage bags full of the rattle of aluminum cans. A plastic bucket ran through with a rake handle. And boxes and boxes and boxes. We counted one, two, THREE and flipped the deep-freezer back right-side up. An electrical cord was passed in through the broken window, the generator was fired up, and the vegetables were salvaged.

Someone from town had brought coffee and breakfast and we took a minute's break to eat and look at the damage to the house. Vinyl siding hung from its walls like the flaking skin of an onion. The front porch overhang sagged askew as its support beams dangled without level purchase to the ground. Shingles were peeled back, some were littered about the lawn. And the whole house was plastered with flecks of green, brown, orange, yellow, the Indian-rainbow; wind-driven leaves and blades of grass.

Someone made a half-hearted joke about tearing the house down and building a new one but no one laughed, not even the one that said it.

By the time we finished with our biscuit-and-tenderloins, the drizzle was gone and the sun was out. We used a car jack and long pieces of lumber to lift the front porch overhang enough to reset the support beams. As we stepped back to appreciate our work, the aunt that had run off to the city finally arrived with more coffee and more breakfast. We all got a laugh in at her expense, partly because of her lateness and partly because of how funny she looked in her brand new polka-dotted galoshes.

The tractor shed had the better part of a tree laid atop it, the tractor itself the only thing keeping it from being pancake flat. We wrapped a stout chain around a corner post and winched the shed up long enough to back the tractor out, its big-tread tires mashing diagonal lines into the soft mud. Then we let it tumble to the ground and we stared down at its mossy shingle roof, wiped the sweat from our foreheads.

Downed trees were everywhere, twisted and splintered and snapped. The blazing ball of the sun was full up as we gassed up the chainsaws, everyone sharing in a laugh at how small mine was. But no matter the size, it made fine work of the cutting and we had at it for hours amongst the octopus arms of the fallen trees. Then we stopped for a bite of Grandmother's homemade sandwiches and sweet iced tea.

A man came from the local paper to take pictures. He said he typically covered sports but this was all-hands-on-deck. He smiled an underbite, motioned toward my Cubs hat, and asked me how I felt. I told him I'd feel a lot better with some middle relief in the pen and we both shook our heads the way only true Cub-fans can. Then I laid out the damage in as clear language as I could and he jotted down shorthand notes on a pocket pad.

Once he left, we went back to the chainsaws and the task of hauling away the endless branches. The sun was beginning to lessen but we worked on. By and by, all the other saws began to dysfunction. The crank cord was sheared on my father's, the chain had slipped from its track on my brother's. But mine kept on keeping on and in the relative silence of its idling engine, I reminded them all of how they'd laughed and we laughed some more.

At last, the setting sun splashed its purple paint across the western horizon and we put the saws away. An assembly line formed, trailing from the capsized metal shed to the house and boxes of all colors and sizes were passed from person to person up the hill. Christmas boxes mainly, but also boxes of jars, old newspapers, old magazines, old keepsakes. Lawn chairs were unfolded and we plopped down exhausted into them and began to sift through the boxes. Someone found a crystal punch bowl set that was hardly chipped and we served cold coffee from it, toasting the passersby that came sightseeing along the road.

One by one we got up and stretched and knuckled our sore backs. We leaned down and hugged Grandmother. Someone said that it sure was one more whopper of a storm and although everyone else nodded, we all knew the truth. It hadn't been a whopper, this storm. A whopper would have slung the house like this storm had slung the shed. A whopper would have drawn more than the sports columnist from the county paper. A whopper would have broken what we couldn't fix, taken more than we were willing to give. And I think we knew it, all of us.

But no one said it, and that was okay, too.

Then we left, our headlights cutting cones into the night.

From the Backs of
Four Shop-Rite Bags

from the first bag

The hand-painted sheet of cardboard in the window of Shop-Rite bore the words CLOSE-OUT SPECIAL...BARGAIN-LOW PRICES!!! What it did not say was STOCK UP FOR THE END OF THE WORLD or LAST-DAY-ZOMBIE-SALE. Signs like that carried the potential to incite panic and panic could turn to riot and riot in these conditions, with this many folks toting firearms in itchy hands and itchy fingers would be dangerous. As dangerous as what they said was headed our way.

The parking lot was crowded with last minute cars and trucks, but mostly trucks, as the majority of Mississippians, especially small town Mississippians, prefer utility to fuel-efficiency. The vehicles that weren't in motion, U-turning or K-turning, pulling in, pulling out, were idling and as ready to go as a John Dillinger get-away. I glanced into the cab of one such truck and crazy eyes peered back at me like some frightened animal from a hole. I didn't recognize that face but as I moved on, I did see some folks I knew, that I had known for a lifetime, and raised my hand in what passes for a wave in these parts only to get a tight lipped nod from a few. Most just looked back expressionlessly as if I, with dead groping hands, might rip their car doors from their hinges and open their skulls for chili bowls.

The IN-door dinged like always over my left shoulder and there was Bobby Lancaster's smiling face, slightly flushed around the cheekbones where his skin was pushed up.

"We've got good deals today," he said, obstructively kind. "From light bulbs to lighter fluid, tomatoes to tortillas. And the canned goods of course."

Bobby had never met customers at the door before but this was a day for never-befores.

"Okay Bobby." I tried to shuffle past him. "Thanks."

"I mean it. If you can name it, we got it. And for cheap. And plenty enough for everybody. Pah-lent-tee."

"Okay Bobby."

And I walked off, escaping to my left. Behind me, the door dinged its hollow electric ding and Bobby started in on the same spiel with his next customer, saying out loud what the sign in his front window said only in its readers' minds. And both avoiding the same truth.

I grabbed a cart and wasn't surprised that the back right wheel flopped uselessly when I pushed it as if it couldn't determine whether it was coming or going. Shop-Rite only had hand-me-down carts and this particular model probably hadn't driven true since it swung up and down the aisles of one of the chain grocery mega-joints in Littleton or Martin. As I looked down to kick the wheel into alignment, the smells of cheap perfume and baby powder swept me over.

MaryAnne Gipson had been two grades below me in school. Most freshmen girls would murder to go to the prom with a junior, but not MaryAnne, not with me. She had turned me down colder than witches' breasts. Now as she sped past me and my defunct shopping buggy, her left arm loaded down with a battery value-pack and a precarious tower of canned beans, her right slung around a baby of perhaps six months, I thought about asking her to reconsider. Her man had up and left her with that baby still in her belly instead of on her hip and that was back when survival had meant a completely different thing. But MaryAnne Gipson went right on by, her eyes set on the check-out lines and her attention set on not tumbling her cargo. And I let her, weaving my way over to the egg, cheese, and yogurt cooler.

"Hey!" A shout from my right. "What the heck-o are you doing?"

I spun around and up aisle two stood Maude and Clutch McBeene, my Pops's old railroad buddies and, besides me, the only two mourners at his funeral last spring. Maude had me sighted with a scowl that passed for her look of concern. There was a rifle in her fist.

"Stocking up, I guess."

She waved her free hand. "No, I don't mean what are you *doing*-doing. I mean what the H-E-double-L are you doing un-fricking-armed?"

I looked at her rifle. It was a relic of a World War and looked capable of felling a woolly mammoth. Then I looked down at my own hands. One rested flaccidly on the buggy handle with the words SHOP-RITE OR DON'T SHOP AT ALL stenciled over the original proprietor's name and logo. The other clutched a dozen large eggs.

She spoke as she stalked towards me, Clutch following along behind like a dog tethered to the bumper of a slow-rolling automobile. "Look-here, you see this fricking crap?" She snatched my carton of eggs and waved it in front of my face. "Worthless. If it has to be kept cold, it'll ruin before you can eat it. Power'll be gone soon, you can bet on it. So if it's stocking up you're here for, fill that buggy with bottled water and something canned. Maybe bags of rice. Jerky. Anything with big expiration dates and minimal prep. That's short for prep-are-a-tion. Use your fricking head." She slammed the eggs down and I heard a crunching-squishing sound as every yolk in my carton and the one below it was introduced to the outside world.

Behind Maude, the puppy caught up with the car and nodded at me.

"Clutch," I said and nodded back.

Clutch's eyes were downcast and he shook his head. "Dad-blamed zombies," he muttered to the floor and me. "The dad-blamed mother-truckin' undead, can you believe it?"

Maude McBeene, the murderer of at least twenty-four unborn chickens, rounded on him. "Yeah and what are *you* gonna do? Fricking hurl curses at 'em?" I saw that Clutch's hands were as empty as mine. Maude turned back to me, the ammunition belts crisscrossed over her flannel shirt sparkling with brassy reflections of Bobby Lancaster's fluorescents. "Look-here, you need to get cowboyed up with some iron and ammo once you finish up here. No two ways about it, you hear? I suggest a rifle, high caliber if'n you can place a hand on one -"

"Now hang on just a second." Clutch's voice sounded full of timid certainty. "He never said he *wanted* to tote a gun, Maude. Matter of fact, I reckon that if that's what he wanted, he'd just scoot on down to Paulie's and buy one for hisself. You gotta stop projecting yourself onto everybody around you." Then he got more timid than certain. "I love you, sis, but you do."

Maude's breath pulled in and her knuckles turned white around her own piece of iron that had no more come from Paulie's Sporting Goods than Adolf Hitler had come from Utah. "Projecting? What are you, fricking Sigmund Freud? This ain't projecting Clutchey. Heck-o, it's just being fricking smart. These things are coming and if they don't get *shot*," she shook her gun and the shells inside rattled like a baby's toy, "they will kill you in a fricking atrocious manner. Now, if being breakfast for some moaning, foot-dragging, slack-jawed, fricking dead-undead *goon* sounds fine by you, well then..." She spread her arms in a surrendering cruciform. "But if you'd rather stay alive and uneaten, like me, then I suggest you get over your gun-phobia and arm yourself with more than just a load of that pacifist-psychology-hogwash." She spun back towards me with a pointed finger. "That goes for you too, buddy."

There was a moment of awkwardness in which I watched yellow goo glop out of the busted egg cartons and onto the tile floor. Folks passed us by like a shallow stream around three boulders. You could feel the tense terror radiating off them like a brush fire that could catch wind and be out of control in an instant. Finally, I looked back up at the McBeenes.

"What's your..." I floundered but there was only one word for it really. "What's your plan, Maude?" Clutch looked up and caught my eyes before trailing them back to the floor. I nodded. "Clutch."

Under his breath. "Dad-blamin' cannot believe...dad-blame Saturday night horror flick zombies..."

He was ignored by his sister who leaned in close enough for me to lay out the complete menu of her previous three feedings by smell alone. The thought drew me back to the crushed eggs, but, to stave off an intense wave of nausea, I didn't dare look.

"See all these other folks?" She paused and we scanned around at all the scurrying little ants, gathering stores and scurrying, scurrying, scurrying. "Most of these folks are going to ground. Storm shelters and the like. And that's alright if this thing don't turn to fighting, but me? I'd rather see what's coming."

I looked to Clutch for help but all I made eye contact with were the age-spots showing through the wisps of gray that still clung hopelessly to his scalp.

"What are you talking about?" I asked. "I don't follow."

"I'm talking about high ground. Tactical fricking advantage. I'm talking about not being trapped down in some cellar like a mole in a hole." She startled me then by hoisting her rifle and peering down the barrel at as-yet unseen creatures. "I'm talking about fricking picking these gut-bags off one by one. Putting a slug of lead in anyone or any *thing* that makes toward me or my kin, even if all that amounts to is my half-wit Clutchey."

"Okay, someplace high up. You got a place like that?"

"Sure do. Muddy Pine Ridge. I do my deer hunting up there and I've got a stand. It's one of those industrial-sized jobs big enough for three persons and supplies and what-not. So we're getting what we need - *what will last* - and then we're picking up Clutch's pressure medicine at Baxter's and hiking up there before...well, before you know." After a moment's contemplation, she looked over at Clutch and nodded. "You wanna be our third guy? If'n you ain't got nowhere else?"

I didn't. Have anywhere else, that is. Embarrassingly enough, my plan was to get eggs, milk, and bread and then go back to my trailer and lock the door. Maybe board up the windows if things got hairy. In the stark clarity of hindsight, I realize I would have been dead or worse by moonrise that first night. But before I could answer, and as if summoned magically by the mere mention of his name, Doug Baxter walked by and Maude's attention shifted.

"Dougie, hey Dougie!" she called.

He turned and his eyes looked as empty as clay jars. They weren't panicked eyes and they weren't zombie eyes; they were well past the former and drawing nearer to the latter.

"Doug, is the drug store closed? We've got something to get filled. Clutchey's pressure pills. We want to buy as much of them pills as you got and don't give me no hogwash about not having enough refills or insurance or any of that."

Two summers ago, I had an abscessed tooth. A back molar. It felt like someone had stabbed my gums with something pointy but not quite sharp, like a pie server. Repeatedly. The pain was such that I didn't flinch at going to a high-dollar dentist over in Littleton to get it seen about. I'll never forget the sideways way Doug Baxter had looked first at my pain prescription and then at me. That sideways glare had a way of making you feel like a drug-seeking criminal even if all you wanted was for the pain to stop for twenty minutes so you can eat a meal consisting of something other than mashed potatoes.

But this Doug Baxter was devoid of that sideways-ness. Maybe devoid of everything else too.

"Eddie Dill from the parts store said his cousin saw them," he said, his voice sounding far away and oddly unconcerned. "Coming up from Martin. I asked him was he sure, that the news said they's coming down. *Down* the east coast, *down, down.* That would give us a day at the least, maybe more with luck. But Eddie said he's sure. *Up* from Martin. So there's really no time at all."

Doug stared off into the pallet of colors on the produce aisle. Maude's eyes danced as her mind no doubt raced through scenarios and poor one-track Clutch mumbled about dad-blamin' zombies walking north from the county seat.

"Door's open," the pharmacist continued. "I propped it back with a cement block. The shelves are alphabetical from left to right. Take what you need if it's still there, Maude." Then he nodded and muttered, "Clutch." And he stalked away.

Just then Bobby Lancaster came jogging up. His smile was gone, replaced by a 12-gauge side-by-side laid over his forearm. He looked like a frantic pheasant hunter.

"You folks hear the news? They're closer'n we thought. Eddie Dill's cousin spotted 'em -"

"Yeah Bobby, thanks. We know."

"Good. Okay, good." He hefted his shotgun and seemed surprised that it was still there. "We've got a pretty good set up here. I sent Biggers and some of the boys out for lumber to board up the front windows. We've got food and drink and a generator and radios and you-name-it-we-got-it. Figured we'd make a go of it right here." His eyeballs swelled when they fell on Maude's rifle. "You three are welcome to pitch in with us."

Maude shook her head and her jowls jiggled unflatteringly. "Thanks Bobby, but zombies or no zombies and Clutchey here'll die without his prescription. And we've gotta plan after we go to Baxter's to pick it up. Ain't that right Clutchey?"

Clutch's face said the prospect of hunkering down at Shop-Rite with its abundance of you-name-its appealed to his better senses. But his sister was a trump card, had been ever since he could remember, and she was lying face up and staring at him.

"Clutch, answer the man," Maude said sternly.

Clutch nodded and looked back at the floor between his bow-legged feet.

"How's about you, son?" Lancaster said and I realized he was talking at me. "You with them?"

I had no immediate answer. In my mind, I was up on Muddy Pine Ridge, spooning cold pinto beans from a can with two hooked fingers, watching silently as the hoards of undead flowed along beneath us, picking off the few that lifted their eyes usward. Then, I was in Shop-Rite. The lights pulsed weakly as the gennie roared from some unseen place behind me. The sound of glass shattering. Impacts on the makeshift plywood barriers. The volume of the moans rising with each collective fist bang like the bleep of a dying EKG.

Neither was attractive. But I'd hunted up on Muddy Pine Ridge, too and foxholing with my fellow Shop-Rite patrons seemed a little too Stephen King for my tastes.

"Yeah." My voice. I guess I'd made my decision. "I'm with them."

Maude exuded as much satisfied vindication as her face would allow and her brother looked perfectly dismayed. The female McBeene came alongside me and my buggy and spoke her breath into my face again.

"We need to hurry," she said. "If you can drive this thing, I'll fill it up. Bobby, where do you keep the fricking Moon-pies?"

from the second bag

Main Street was deserted and Baxter's had been looted.

The cement block was there just like Dougie had said, but there were also glittering diamonds of broken glass on the sidewalk from where someone had put another such brick through the front picture window seemingly for the thrill of it. Greeting cards and envelopes fluttered out through the open doorway like a bevy of released pigeons. Even the shingle out front that read BAXTER'S DISCOUNT DRUGS---YOUR FAMILY RX SHOPPE hung on a vicious slant from its one remaining chain.

The McBeenes's four-wheel drive Scout, newly loaded down with crinkling paper grocery sacks in the back, me riding shotgun, and the McBeenes themselves, puttered up to the curb. Maude threw the shifter up into park. Then, she leaned back and watched Baxter's with a gunslinger's steely eye.

"You're with me," she said at last, pushing open her rusty hinged door and curling a fist around her gun. "Clutchey, you stay with the supplies."

Clutch never budged from the back seat where he sat drinking a grape soda and munching on a Moon-Pie. It was his second in less than ten minutes.

I got out and followed Maude into the pharmacy. We were greeted by the cool of air conditioning and Alan Jackson's *Way Down Yonder on the Chattahoochee* twanging on the overheads.

"Something ain't right here."

Maude firmed her rifle's stock up on her shoulder and puckered her left eye. I wanted to ask if that was a reference to the broken teeth yawn of Dougie's front window, the general disarray of the store, or the quality of Alan's earlier work, but then I heard a rattling coming from behind the counter and my unspoken question was answered. What wasn't right was that the looting was not a done deal. It was still in progress.

Maude hitched her head in the rattling's direction; code for follow-me-this-way. I waved my hand and bobbed my own noggin in the silent reply of you-go-ahead-I'll-be-right-behind-you-remember-you-have-the-gun.

As we walked over the litany of unshelved gift store crapola towards the business end of Baxter's, the canned Alan Jackson changed over to canned Marty Robbins and now we were true gunslingers and Millwood Branch was the West Texas town of El Paso.

The rattling came in spurts and as we drew closer, we could make out muttered curses between each series of rattles. *"...fudgin', dumpin', mother-truckin' open...gull-dern-it now open,* OPEN..." Followed by more rattling, as rapid as machine gun fire but not as loud.

We walked past the PICK UP LINE BEGINS HERE...PRIVACY IS OUR POLICY sign. The cash register drawer was out and empty, even the pennies. The mini-refrigerator's door swung lazily on its hinges, vials of insulin lay crushed or up-ended on its shelves and in a rough semicircle around it. Medication stock bottles littered everywhere. And at the far end of the behind-the-counter area, on his knees in front of the locked cabinet from which the original sideways skeptical Doug Baxter, RPh had re-

trieved the pills that had stayed the stabbing pie-server pain of my
hopelessly abscessed molar, was the muttering rattler himself.

"...*mother of all things holy...why don't you just be a good crappety-
crap-crap and open, open, OPEN...*"

Maude had him sighted with that steely right eye straight
down the barrel of her elephant gun but he was too busy jerking
on the locked cabinet door to realize he was dead to rights until
she spoke.

"Shut your filthy mouth and reach for the rafters before you
turn to face me..." She snuck a quick peek over at me. "I mean
'us'."

The rattling stopped, the muttering curses, too. Over our
heads, Marty was paying his last visit to Rosa's Cantina. The
looter removed his hand from the cabinet where he had been
pulling for all he was worth and then some and raised his hands
like a scarecrow. Then he knee-walked around to face us.

"Denny?"

I had gone to junior college with Denny Beck. We were good
friends, not good enough to split text books or car pool, but just
short of that. Certainly if he had a drug problem I would have
heard of it. And the cherry-top was the fact that Denny Beck was
Doug Baxter's brother-in-law. Denny's sister had become Doug's
second wife years ago, so technically speaking, Denny was rob
bing his own kin. I guess nothing blurs the lines of familial loy-
alty quite like the impending doom of a gruesome death.

"Denny, what are you doing?"

His face turned incredulous. "What does it look like I'm doing? Most of the Okay Stuff's already been taken so I'm trying to
get to the Really Good Stuff. In the lock-up. What are *you* doing?"

It was Maude who answered. "*We* are getting *medication*. For
blood pressure. And then we are going to leave Dougie enough
cash to cover it and then we are leaving. You, on the other hand,
are leaving right fricking now." She puckered that left eye and
there was no doubt who she was looking at with her right one.

But Denny ignored the threat. In fact, he looked like a bright idea had just struck him.

"Hey," he said, drawing out the word. "Reckon that gun could bust this mother-humping lock? I bet it will. Say, if you'd go all Calamity Jane on this here lock I'll go halfsies on what's inside."

"I'll do no such."

"Oh, come on."

"No. Doug Baxter is a friend of mine so no."

Denny threw his hands down and punched out his lower lip like a child throwing a tantrum. He kicked at a stock bottle and didn't catch it squarely. It spun below him, mockingly non-habit-forming.

"Puh-*lease*, you guys!" Denny pleaded. "You know what they say is coming, right? I don't want to be coherent when they pull *me* apart, do you? I've heard Doug talk about the euphoria these pills can cause and I WANT ME SOME OF THAT, OKAY? Is that so wrong? Is that so *criminal*? I don't even care if I take so much it kills me. Seems a better way to go, doesn't it?" Then, his final plea to Maude, the one with the cabinet's key wedged against her shoulder and pointed dead between his eyes. "You shoot out that lock and I'll just get what I need and you can help yourself to the rest. I won't even tell Doug if you don't pay."

She lowered her rifle and put a bullet in the floor between Denny's feet. The pharmacy rang like a bell and poor Denny jumped like a jackrabbit on crack. Maude bolted the rifle and had it re-shouldered in a blur.

"Go."

Denny didn't move but to look down in shame at the puddle of urine spreading out on the floor around his sneakers. Maude squeezed off another round that ricochetted off the floor near the first and ended up somewhere in the back and that's when it occurred to me that she might actually kill him.

"Now," she said pulling back on the bolt and slamming it home deliberately, "or the next one will be four feet higher."

Denny reached down to grab an unzipped back pack. The white lids of pharmacy bottles protruded from its opening, no doubt containing all the Okay Stuff he could find.

"Leave it."

Denny whimpered like a whipped hound but he left it. His shoes squished in his bladder's leavings as he left. Never before had I seen a more sullen person.

"Now," Maude said once the squishing had trailed off and we were all alone. "It's called metoprolol tartrate which is a pretty stupid name for anything if'n you ask me, especially something that old folks' lives depend on, but never-mind all that. Let's just find it and get gone.

And so we did. We found enough metoprolol tartrate to regulate Clutch's pressure until Armageddon, which might have been right around the corner for all we knew.

And we got gone.

from the third bag

Muddy Pine Ridge lay just on the western edge of town in an undeveloped area the Two Forks folks thought was theirs. A few years back, the town's aldermen pegged Muddy Pine Ridge as a potential site for a new industrial park. They got as far as running power lines and water mains out there to the north side of the highway before the collective Two Fork's voice shouted its disapproval. The endeavor was halted. But in addition to the pipes that had never held water and the wires that had never hummed with electricity, there was an access road that had barely borne an automobile. The Scout made it almost a mile up that road before a downed tree blocked our path and forced us to stop. Almost a mile, but each and every inch was one I had expected to hike, so I can't say I was disappointed.

Maude: "Get out, Clutchey. Grab something."

Clutch, around a mouthful of something salty, pretzels I think: "Get out? We there?"

"There's a tree. Fricking wake up."

So we each got an armful. Clutch and I had two grocery sacks apiece and Maude toted the bottled water and of course, big iron.

"Sorry we didn't have time to get you cowboyed up," she huffed.

"That's alright. Hopefully we won't need it."

It was a hope of mine but I'm not sure Maude shared it.

"Don't worry," she said as she readjusted the plastic-wrapped case of water on her shoulder. "When we get high and dry, we'll take turns with the rifle. Me first, then you, and then back and forth. Just do not pass it over to Clutchey. Guns make him nervous and he's liable to go into panic mode if he's to touch one. So, just me and you, okay?"

"Alright, sure." There was something bothering me and I wanted to ask it before we got "high and dry" although I guess it was already too late. "Hey, Maude?"

"Yo."

"You think these things can climb? Like trees?"

"Good-gosh no. We're not talking about fricking bears here, okay?" She shot a glance back over her shoulder at her brother who was his typical three steps behind. "And keep your voice down with that talk."

The rest of the walk was quiet and not just because we didn't talk. Whether by means of shock or anticipation, Mother Nature was also hushed. No birds chirped or beat wings in the pine branches. No squirrels scurried in the underbrush. Nothing moved but us. No sounds but for our feet crunching rhythmically through the forest floor. After a while, the silence must've gotten to Clutch because he began to hum out Waylon Jenning's theme to The Dukes of Hazzard, softly at first and rising gradually to full bravado.

We didn't stop him; he carried a decent tune and if the truth be told, the silence was bothering more than just him. Then he started singing the lyrics in addition to humming the interludes and before I knew it, I'd joined right in. Maude, too. And just as we'd begun to tweak out the three part harmonies, we were there.

Maude dropped her waters with a thud and a slosh.

The deer stand was as large and capable as Maude had promised. The platform was bolted to a thick oak about thirty feet up. Camouflage netting hung down from a makeshift roof that consisted of a single sheet of green spray-painted fiberglass laid over a wooden framework. An extension ladder, also bearing a sloppy coat of the green paint leaned against the tree's trunk just below the stand.

The singing stopped and I immediately felt silly for having taken part in it.

"Here we are," Maude said. "High fricking ground, baby."

There was a pause. We all looked up at it, craning our necks, and Clutch and I hefted our loads. We looked down at the awkward bundle of bottled waters. Then we looked back up, following the long line of the ladder with our eyes. I felt like Moses looking over into Canaan.

"Um, sis..."

"What?"

"How're we gonna get all these supplies up there? I mean, mine's kinda heavy."

Maude grinned impishly and spoke where only I could hear. "Same way me and your ole Pops used to do things working on the railroad, God-rest-his-soul." Then she favored me with a wink that was kindhearted, almost motherly, before raising her voice loud enough for us both. "Assembly line, Clutchey. Ass-sem-bull-ee line. And you just volunteered to be at the end of it. Go on and put your sacks down and get your hinnie up there."

Clutch did as ordered. As did I and two minutes later, I took the first paper sack from Maude and twisted to pass it up over my head to her brother. Then, the next sack and the next. It was quiet again and at one point Clutch tried to pick up the Waylon tune again but when no one joined in he shut up. That moment had passed and Maude and I, at least, were not willing to revisit it.

The last sack, containing bags of wild rice and marshmallows, vacuum-sealed packages of beef jerky, a four-roll pack of toilet paper, and a half-eaten bag of pretzels, was passed up. Finally came the waters, which nearly tumbled me from the ladder. It shook and groaned and a sprinkling of crushed tree bark fell to the ground from where it leaned against the oak before I was able to complete my turnabout and pass the God-forsaken water up to Clutch. Below me, Maude swiped her forehead with the back of her arm and took a long cautious look around.

"Alright Clutchey. I'm gonna pass up the rifle now so I can climb. Just grab it here and here and prop it up in the corner of the stand and I'll get it when I get up there, okay?"

"Okay."

She handed the rifle up to me and I grabbed it by the barrel and handed it on up to Clutch. He looked like he'd rather touch a coiled up cobra but he took it, gripping it in the places that Maude had instructed. And the instant he had it leaned up in the back corner of the stand, we heard something.

Something...

At first, it was difficult to pinpoint in the relative stillness of our surroundings. Hard to pinpoint just what it was and just how close.

Something...

Leaves and pine needles crushing softly but decisively. A low roar barely more than a forced whisper. The crushing sounds coming faster now, more frequent.

Something...

Running?

Yes. It was running.

It looked no more than sixteen years old. Blonde hair parted to right. Slim. Athletic. It even wore a black and yellow Martin Track and Field t-shirt. It was the All-American Zombie and it was on Maude before any of us could have said Jack Sprat. It dug into the soft area where Maude's neck became her shoulder. Blood cascaded down her front in a red bib that stretched into an apron.

"Clutchey," she shouted as she tried to use her balled fists to beat it off with no effect. "Shoot him, Clutchey! Fricking shoot,

shoot, shoot!" But Clutch McBeene was nothing more than a frozen face above me, his eyes and mouth wide.

"*Shoot this fricking thing, Clutchey. SHOOT!*" And then the last thing, just before it worked around to her vocal cords, "I'm sorry, Clutchey. Take your medicine." And her voice was gone in a guttural snap.

It was like watching a train wreck, except bloodier, more up-close, more intimately violent and up until that moment, I could not peel my eyes away. Then the undead track star dropped Maude's body in a contorted heap of arms and legs, wrapped its gray-toned hand around a ladder rung just below my feet, and bear or no bear, began to climb.

I have no memory of the rest of my climb, but suddenly I was pulling myself up onto the stand's platform and shoving Clutch aside. The ever-troublesome God-forsaken case of water was in the center of the platform and I tripped over it, sending it nearly over the edge and myself nearly head-first into Maude's gun. I struggled up to my hands and knees. That low roar was growing behind me as the thing had almost reached the top of the ladder. Yelling for Clutch to get-down-by-golly-get-down, I grabbed the gun, thumbed off the safety, and spun around. But I didn't spin all the way around; I couldn't. I tried again, yanking harder this time, to no avail.

To borrow from the late Maude McBeene: The fricking front sight on the fricking rifle was tangled up in fricking camo netting.

Behind me, I heard the flap of a cold gray hand on the platform and a deep-throated groan that seemed to never pause for inhalation.

I pulled; nothing.

I pulled again; a ripping sound and the gun seemed freer by the slightest fraction.

The groan was above me now; the thing was standing. I could feel the vibrations of its footfalls.

One final pull and the gun's weight settled on me completely as the dark green netting ripped. I pinched the hand-sanded wooden stock close to my side with my arm, pointed it in the direction from which I'd come, and squeezed the trigger. The bullet caught it square in the chest, between the R and A of Track, and a big red rose of exploded skin blossomed there. Then it was stumbling backward, pinwheeling its arms on the edge of the platform just before it fell.

I heard a meaty thud from thirty feet below. But that sound, that mindless moan, never stopped. I scrambled over to the platform's edge, this time with the rifle's stock firmly on my shoulder, and watched with one part amazement and one part nauseating certainty as the thing regained its feet. It looked up and saw me with eyes that shouldn't see. Shivering, I pulled back on the gun's bolt and ejected the empty casing. Then I sighted it in the dead center of the thing's forehead, took a deep calming breath, and squeezed the trigger on the exhale.

Click.

I tried again. Click again. The thing began to smile, blood so dark it looked like chocolate syrup dripped from the rising corners of its mouth. I pulled open the bolt and saw that the chamber was empty and then I felt my stomach knot into a cramping fist. Maude's body lay on the forest floor, a crumpled and lifeless gore, with two ammo belts criss-crossing her chest. She might as well have been on the surface of the moon. It, the thing, smiled even wider, its teeth red-stained with Maude's blood. Then it stepped up to the ladder and again began to climb.

"Clutch," I gasped. "Clutch, do you have any bullets? Did she give you any bullets?"

But he didn't hear. Evidently, seeing his big sister eaten alive had proven too much for his ticker. His right hand was death-clutching his left shoulder and his lips were already blue. There were banana Moon-Pie crumbs still on his flannel button-up, but he was gone.

I looked down. It was still coming, still climbing rung by rung by inevitable rung.

There was only one option and it simultaneously saved my life and doomed it. I threw Maude's useless gun aside and sat on the edge of the stand. My heel swung like a pendulum and struck the side of the ladder. Reverberations traveled up my body, chattering my teeth, but I swung again. Again my heel hit the ladder and this time, I felt it shift to the left. Still the thing kept climbing. Its groaning had turned into bad-humored laughter and deep in the distance of Muddy Pine Ridge, obscured by the leafy boughs of the forest, I heard that laughter echoed countless times over.

I raised my foot and swung again, screaming in terror and pain and effort as my heel impacted the steel of the ladder. There was a scrape of metal on wood and the slightest touch of a finger on my sneaker and the ladder was falling. Falling, falling, falling; the only way they could reach me, the only way I could escape.

from the last bag

That first night I worked. I pulled down all the netting and braided it into rope. Then, I attached my belt on the end. It was as close to a grapple as I could manage. But when the dawn arrived, Maude's body was gone. Whether it was carried away in the darkness by the creatures or became a creature and simply stood up and walked off, I do not know. However it went, it carried the ammunition with it, robbing my makeshift grapple of a purpose.

That very morning, I said a fittingly simple goodbye to Clutch and dropped him over the edge out of fear that whatever was causing this, whatever *they* had, was contagious and airborne. Like his sister, his body was gone by midday.

After that point, I began to lose all sense of the passage of time. I ate and drank as little as possible. I dozed in short fitful nightmarish spans. I relieved myself over the edge of the platform. I hummed old country and western tunes to drown out the moaning monsters beneath me. And I thought.

In the beginning, my thoughts centered around things I had no control over. I thought about the folks holed up at Shop-Rite and when I began to feel envious of them, I was careful to remind myself that there was no reason to suspect that they were fairing any better. I thought about the crystalline structure of the world, of the governments from local to state to federal. I thought about the National Guard. I thought about the Marines. I thought about survival of the fittest and I thought about the lack of helicopters beating the air over my head.

I thought about the destruction of a species.

Sometimes I would become so lost in my thinking, I would see the faces of people I knew in the dead faces passing below me. I saw MaryAnne Gipson and her baby, the former still carrying the latter. Except they weren't alive, they were *them*. Gray skin, blood smattered mouths that gaped at odd angles, and eyes with no life behind them. Then I blinked and they were gone. But they never *stayed* gone. Sometimes it was Dougie Baxter or Denny Beck or even good ole Bobby Lancaster groping up at me. Sometimes it's names I can't remember but faces I've seen around town. Once I even saw myself, whether by premonition or delirium, I cannot be sure.

As time wore on, I thought less and less about the big picture and began to work out what I would do when my meager supply of eats and drinks ran out.

I thought about metoprolol tartrate and how much it would take to kill a man. More than once, I poured out a handful of the oblong peach tablets and considered knocking it back and washing them down with the last of the bottled water. But I've heard that some drugs kill you slow and I didn't know enough about Clutch's pressure pills to give it a try. So I always dumped the pills back into the bottle.

The culmination of all my thinking was that it would need to be quick and a sure thing, so there was really only one option.

I had a rope thanks to my first night's efforts, and if you're reading this you already know that my plan was not to use it to climb down; not down there, not ever. The fiberglass roof of the deer stand is brittle and weatherworn but the wood frame that it's bolted to appears sturdy enough to support my weight.

As a postscript, I would advise against cutting me down. The dead cannot be trusted.

Goodnight Young Miss Lana Jones

one

It all started the night after the funeral.

Lana left the black dress on until just before bedtime. She locked the doors and drew the curtains in it. She flipped off the living room and kitchen lights in it. She wore it as she washed her makeup off and brushed her teeth. The dress was new, bought that very morning at a small boutique in Littleton called B's Bliss. It still smelled like the cardboard box she had brought it home in. She had never owned a black dress and it didn't remind her of anything, so she left it on. But she knew she couldn't sleep in it. Her normal sleep clothes, her gowns and his old soft t-shirts, all carried too many memories. And so just before clicking off her bedside lamp, she slipped the dress over her head and hung it on the bathroom doorknob by one of its shoulder straps and she slipped herself between the bedsheets, naked as if she were stepping into a cool shower.

The moment the light was out and she was settled, Donnie propped up on an elbow. Lana always slept on the side away from the windows and his silhouette was a perfect thing in the moonlight let in by the blinds. She could feel his breaths flexing the mattress springs beneath her. The heat of his body. The smell of his nightly Pabst.

"I reckon you should stay home t'morrow."

She thought for a moment and then decided to answer.

"I need to go."

He looked over at her now. His features were lost in shadow but he was looking at her.

"That school can get on just as well without you. Maybe not a long time. Maybe not a week even, but it'll do for a day or two."

"No, I need to go for me."

Donnie shook his head but he let it be. His soft brown curls threw back only enough of the moon to keep from being full black. With that thought, Lana reflexively spared a glance at the funeral dress that hung halfway down the bathroom door. It hung there limply, swallowing up the moonlight, a black hole that threatened to devour her too. For a moment, she felt its pull, felt it grow like the approaching mouth of a dark tunnel. The smell of PBR brought her back around.

"I reckon I'd be right in saying there ain't no talking you out of it. I've seen mules with less determination."

She cocked an eyebrow. "Mules?"

"None of them was as pretty, 'course."

Lana couldn't see his smile, but she heard it in his voice. It was that one-sided smile that crept up when he was being flirty. In spite of the circumstances, she blushed. True, it was a small little thing but Donnie always did the small little things just right.

"Just do me one favor, would you?"

She said she would.

"Tomorrow morning, go the other way, down by the old tractor shop. And come home that away t'morrow afternoon, too."

Before she even thought about it, her mouth opened to say that would add time to her drive, ten maybe fifteen minutes and that's assuming she didn't get in behind a school bus. Which, on that stretch of road, at those times of the day, she probably would.

"Hush," Donnie said, interrupting her before she began. "Go the other way and that's the end of it. You forget. I can be a mule, too."

And then she smiled, hoping he was seeing her smile. But even if he wasn't she imagined he knew, the same way she had.

In the shadows, he looked around, took a few deep breaths that made tiny pops in the mattress springs below them. He brought a hand to his mouth and yawned into it. It was almost time for him to sign off and roll over toward the window, toward the moonlight. But before he did, he looked at her again. Lana couldn't see, but she knew he winked. And that one side of his face was smiling.

"Sure were pretty tonight."

"Which do you mean," she asked, "mule-pretty or pretty-pretty?"

"You know which."

Then he turned slowly away from her. His smells, the smell of his soap, the faintest trace of sawed wood, his one nightly beer, those smells crashed on her like the wind of a spring storm and then were swept away just as quickly. His head settled on his pillow. His curls browned by the moon's ghostly glow.

"Good night young Miss Lana Jones."

And before she had another thought, she was asleep and that first night after his funeral was passing her by.

two

She turned off the highway and as she had feared, fell right in behind Coach Bingham's bus. Its rear windows were caked with layers upon layers of back road dust, the black lettering nearly fading into the yellow background. There was the hiss of air-brakes as the bus eased to a halt and a red-lit stop sign swiveled out from its side.

Lana peeked around the bus's back-left corner and then checked the digital clock in her Mercury's dashboard. She would be well ahead of the tardy-bell and even the five-minute-warning-bell, but Lana had a very strict self-imposed punctuality standard that eclipsed those of the school employee handbook and by those, she was on the verge of being late. She peered around the bus again, past the stop sign hinged to its side, past Bingham's elbow jutted comfortably out the driver's side window, past the rusted-out eyesore of the old tractor shop, and saw five, maybe six mailboxes standing like sentries along the left hand side of the road. She was unable to see how many stood in likewise fashion on the opposing side of the road, but she estimated a similar number.

The slap of a screen door brought her attention around. It was the Howard boy sprinting toward the bus, smiling that little gremlin smile of his. His little sister - Lana couldn't call her first name at that moment if a gun had been pointed at her head but knew she was in Ms. Pam's kindergarten and that, according to Pam, she was already smarter than her brother would ever be - she was a small forgotten thing on the doorstep, sucking down the dust kicked up by her brother's mad dash down the driveway. The little girl batted her eyelids and squinted at the bus and wafted her pudgy hand in front of her face. Lana heard a muffled but unified exultation from the children inside the yellow belly of the bus as Ty Howard joined them, no doubt sharing his latest and greatest stupid human trick or the newest dirty word gleaned from his father's voluminous vocabulary of dirty words. Meanwhile, Coach Bingham's arm was hung out of the window, waving big circles through the air, imploring Little Nameless Howard to hurry, but she was determined to take her precious time. She waited for the dust to settle, then she hitched up her backpack, bent and grabbed a plastic lunchbox, and took two steps before realizing the laces on her white sneakers had come untied. As she dropped to one knee and attended to her shoe, Lana shot one more glance at the clock.

Five mailboxes. Maybe six. And that was just on one side of the road.

She dropped the Mercury into reverse and K-turned her way back out to the highway.

"I won't look, Donnie."

But of course when she got to the four-way, she did look. It was impossible not to, even with extraordinary effort. And, in truth, she tried very little.

Diamonds of broken glass, pieces too small to be called shards. Bits of plastic, of metal. All right there in the middle of the intersection. Right there where you were forced to drive over them or around them, forced to hear your tires crunch on the remains of it all or consciously avoid it, neither of which offered to ease the thoughts billowing inside Lana's head.

The larger pieces had been pitched out of the way, but only so far as the northwest corner of the intersection, onto a grassy area just beyond the yield ramp. Lana stole a look there and immediately wished she hadn't. A fender, mangled, scraped clean of paint in most places, white in all others. A radiator grill. The half-moon of what was once a hubcap. And a seat, from the truck, foam escaping by way of numerous slashes and punctures, more out than in. Splotches of a dried dark color that could have been anything, but she knew was not.

three

When she was a girl, during moments in which her mother was preoccupied with some man or another, Lana would tip-toe out the back door of their small prefab home, taking care the screen door didn't slap against the jamb behind her. Then, she would follow a narrow gash in the woods behind their house to the place where a runoff created a natural brook. The water was so cool and refreshing on her bare feet and ankles. She didn't care that it was filthy and utterly opaque beyond a depth of one inch. She'd gather her skirts or roll up her jeans and sit in the moss and dangle her legs and let it all just flow her by. For hours she'd sit there, never fully in the water, never fully out. Many times she'd lose her grip on the elusive balloon string of time and not come to until the sun was but red candlelight peeking through the latticework of the treetops, the baying of her mother's car horn calling her home.

That first day flowed her by in much the same way. There were the condolences, a parade of them in fact. The early birds, of which there were few, got theirs in before the first bell. Everyone else paid her small painted cinderblock office the obligatory visit during their planning period, stretching the affair out over the entire course of the day. Lana dipped her feet into these conversations, allowed the mirk to hide her up to the ankle, the lower curve of her calf, but no more.

Through it all was woven the bright crimson thread of normalcy: the hee-haw of middle school children echoing up the long hallway, the intermittent bleep-ring of the telephone, the country-western of her dollar store radio in its place on the window sill. Only a thread, the simplest of stitch, but enough to hold the gray and black patchwork of the day together.

"Mrs. Carmichael?"

Lana shook herself. The recitation of *He Stopped Loving Her Today* filled her little office and somewhere between the George Jones and the whir of the window-unit fighting valiantly against the early September heat, she'd lost herself.

"Lana. Are you alright, sweetheart?"

The voice belonged to Ms. Hale. And there she stood in the office doorway; an even five feet six, lumberjack build, coal-black eyes looking over the tops of two scoops of red-plastic framed lenses low on her nose. The same as when Lana herself had been a fifth grader, excepting a few more frown lines around the mouth and white streaks in the hair.

Ms. Hale cleared her throat. She lowered her chin to her chest and gazed even higher over her readers. The corner of one side of her mouth pinched up in the same don't-you-mess-with-me-buddy way Lana remembered from grade school.

"Mrs. Carmichael, that was what we call an interrogative sentence. 'Are you alright, sweetheart?' Now, although I am admittedly rather out of touch with contemporary communication norms, what with all the OMGs and BFFs and you know you know you knows and whatnots, I believe it remains proper etiquette to respond to interrogatives with a reply of some sort?"

During this, Lana involuntarily folded her hands in her lap and straightened her spine. With effort, she reminded herself that she and Edwina Hale were coworkers now.

"Yes, Ms. Hale," she said. "Fine. I am fine. Just..."

"Just chasing butterflies in the meadow of your mind. I am, as you may imagine, quite familiar with the look."

Lana couldn't help it. She lowered her eyes. A whooped puppy avoiding the gaze of its master.

"Yes, ma'am," she said, somewhere between a croak and a whisper.

"Well, there is no need in dolling it up, now is there? You have good reason to be less than chipper today of all days. Shouldn't even be here in my opinion but what would I know about it? I've never lost a husband because I never found one in the first place. One might argue over which is the worse but that argument might be better had at some later date, yes? The fact of the matter is you *are* here and, from what I can tell, Mr. Darlington is not. Out to the district office I presume?" Ms. Hale raised one eyebrow. Although she didn't place finger quotation marks around her words, she might as well have. Everyone knew the elementary school principal wasn't really at the district office each day when he left the campus shortly after second lunch returned to their classrooms. The assumption, and a correct one, was that a combination of a spastic colon and a staunch unwillingness to use the boy's restroom down the hall forced Mr. Darlington to drive to his house out in Two Forks for a fifteen minute hiatus each day.

Lana checked the clock on her desk and was shocked at the speed with which the afternoon was passing her by. "Yes, ma'am," she said. "This is his normal district office time." Lana didn't use finger quotes either, but they both knew they were there.

Ms. Hale straightened herself and cleared her throat. "Very well," she said. Then she reached beyond the doorframe and produced a child - a mousy little thing named Evie Sue Sistern - and with both hands placed firmly on the peaks of the child's boney shoulders, thrust her into Lana's office. "Young Miss Sistern here," continued Ms. Hale in that same haute tone with which Lana was all too familiar, "is feeling ill. She is unable, so she claims, to continue with her studies today and I am inclined to agree. If it is catching, I cannot bear to have the whole of fifth grade preoccupied with matters of health during direct and indirect objects. Under normal circumstances, I would ask Mr. Darlington to watch over this matter until the elder Miss Sistern can pick up her child, which will be after the end of her shift at the plant as she has told me on more than one occasion that she cannot afford to miss any more work without the fear of termination, but as we have already stated, he is not on the premises."

A grin bloomed on Lana's face and then blossomed further at her sudden realization of its genuineness and its innocence. A smile. She could smile.

"I'd be glad for the company," she said to Ms. Hale, then turning her focus on the child, "We'll just hang out for a little while until your mom can get here won't we, Evie Sue?"

The little girl's eyes wouldn't meet Lana's. They danced around the room, flitting here and there, but never settling in one particular place for too long as if they were following an unseen mosquito or house fly. "It's just Evie," the fifth grader said. "Evie Sue sounds like somebody on one of those reality shows about rednecks."

Lana nodded slowly. "I see."

Meanwhile, Ms. Hale had turned her hips and when she spoke to Lana, she did so with her chin cocked back on her shoulder. "You'll be fine then. Now, if you don't mind Mrs. Carmichael, I'd best return to my classroom ere the fear of my returning has faded from their little minds."

And with that, she was gone, leaving the office to only Lana, the long-ago vocals of Travis Tritt, and Evie Sue. Or rather, Evie.

four

"Okay. Go on. I'm still listening."

Oh, how Lana wanted to run her hands through those curls. Feel their fineness give way to coarse as her fingers combed over his ear to the nape of his neck. How she wanted to reach out, across that vast ocean between them and wrap some part of herself around him. To touch and to feel and to know. To hold and be held.

But we can't always get what we want.

Donnie would have said that. In fact, he probably would have sung it.

So Lana had paused a moment and looked. Let her eyes do what her hands could not.

Without her realizing it, her mind had dived from the solid ground of the present and began swimming in the pool of the past. Them sitting cross-legged in the hallway at school, Lana feverishly doing his algebra homework in the waning seconds before the second bell despite his best efforts to make her laugh. Another day, night. Donnie, his sweaty baseball jersey still on from the game and a can of dollar store spray paint in his hand, hollering for her to put the high-beams on in his truck as his boots crunched on Bullfrog Road gravel, her sliding across the bench-seat all the while craning her head around for blue-lights. The ceremony that June, memories almost too bright to see. The drive home after, the sunlight painting them in smiles.

Donnie's shadow shifted. His elbow propped him up and his head cocked her way.

"Were you planning on finishing this story tonight?" he asked, shocking her out of her reverie. "Or are you gonna leave me with a cliffhanger?"

"Oh yeah," she said, trying to reestablish herself in the here and now. "Where was I?"

"You and this kid in your office."

"Right. So we sit there for a while and I keep on working, still putting kindergarteners into the system, and the phone rings a few times of course and I deal with that and all the while poor Evie Sue is just sitting in the corner with her head down and when I remember that she's there, which is easy to forget because she's being so still and quiet, but when I remember her, I ask her how she's doing. Is she feeling alright, you know?"

"Yeah."

He always listened well, Donnie. Always asked her about her day and always listened. He wouldn't say much and he'd never interrupt, but he'd pepper in a comment here and there to let her know he was still there.

He's still there.

She nearly reflexed into the past again. All the late night conversations. All the how-was-your-days. His yeahs and go-ons. All the smells, the Pabst, the oak, the cedar. The shadows. The moonlight.

"Well, she never lets her head up," Lana continued. "I just hear her voice say 'I'm existing'. Every time I ask, that's her answer. 'I'm existing, Mrs. Carmichael. I'm existing'.

"Existing?"

"Right. Existing. That's all she'd say to me."

"Hmmm." Donnie's head nodded slowly. "Okay. Weird...but, okay."

"Yes," she agreed. "Anyway, this went on for a while. Only God knows what's taking Mr. Darlington so long - I'm not sure I *want* to know - and then that's when it happened.

five

The overhead lights browned out. The window unit set into an abbreviated fuss of warbles and hiccups before going completely dead. Randy Travis's *Forever and Ever Amen* came to an abrupt end on the radio. Lana looked up from her desk. Evie Sue Sistern's head was still down, her hair hanging loose like damp laundry on a line, but her voice came through clear in the sudden silence.

"The gift of time is not lightly given."

six

"'The gift of time is not lightly given.'? Is that what you said?"

"No. That's what I said *she* said."

"'The gift of time...'" Donnie leaned his head back and appeared to work it over in his mind. Lana could see this hair fall away from his brow, the sharp point of his throat against the faint light of the window. "'The gift of time...'"

The bedroom grew silent and the silence carried a heavier weight on the heels of such a lengthy and thought provoking account. Lana watched the silhouette between her and the window, measuring it for a reaction. At last, his head raised, the quietly thrumming cord of tension strung between them relaxed and he spoke. "And then what happened?"

"Then nothing," she replied. "The lights came back on. Radio and computer and air conditioner and everything all at once. Nearly gave me a heart attack. I was too shocked to ask Evie Sue what exactly she had meant and before I knew it, Mr. Darlington was back and the day carried on and although I'm sure her mother came in at some point and signed Evie Sue out, I couldn't tell you exactly when. I just got busy and swept away and all of a sudden, the day was done and I was home. I had actually forgotten all about it until just now."

"Hmmm. What do you think she meant by it?"

Lana actually hadn't forgotten about Evie Sue's episode until that night. In fact, her mind had dwelt on it all afternoon. That phrase. Spoken like some sort of prophesy in a fantasy novel. Several times, she had considered calling Gena Sistern and asking to speak to her daughter to find out just that. What she had meant by it. But Lana had a deep down feeling that even Evie Sue wouldn't know. No more than Lana herself anyway.

"I'd rather hear what you think it means."

At length, Donnie laid back down. His shadow merging with the bed's, his profile a range of cold black mountains. "I think it means a little girl was sick or getting her first period or the epilepsy and that Hickahala Electric was doing some patchwork upstream from the schoolhouse *and*," he added with emphasis, "that you should have taken my advice and stayed home today." He breathed. "That being out and said, I think time *is* a gift. The little girl, for whatever reason she said it, is right. Wondering and figuring on how come a bad thing happened holds you back when you should be moving on. Wondering and figuring on how come a good thing *is* happening keeps you from enjoying it while it's here. Either one's a waste of time."

He turned then and faced the window. Lana herself relaxed and began to flutter her eyes to a close. The sail of slumber had been raised over her now and all that was left was for her to un-moor and allow herself to float away. But before she did, she wanted to ask one more thing. One more thing on the subject and she'd never waste another gifted moment on it.

"Do you think we'll have much time, Donnie? Like this, I mean?"

"We'll have what we'll have, my young Miss Lana Jones. If it was up to me, we'd have forever but I reckon it's not. We'll have what we'll have."

She fell asleep in the best way. Not knowing exactly where the dividing line between yesterday and today, today and tomorrow occurred. The next morning, she woke before her alarm and ran a

cautious hand across the bed. The sheets there were cool and
empty, warmed only by what beams of sunlight the blinds would
allow, but something told her the good thing hadn't passed her
completely by. The moon was waning and would soon be new.
Until then, they would have what they would have.

seven

That Saturday, Donnie's sister came by for a few hours to help go through some of his things. There were his clothes, of course, to be dealt with. His shoes and old work boots. And his tools. Pocketknives, high school baseball trophies, a million odds and ends. A milk crate full of worn Louis L'Amours he had read time and time again, the ink fading from the pages and the paper backings creased and torn. There were even four PBRs remaining in the fridge.

Vanessa cried almost the entire time. She would seem to work her way over an emotional hurdle, swallow back a sob, and rub her cheeks dry, and then a new item would emerge like his CD collection, mostly Hank Williams and Garth Brooks and George Strait, in a black zippered binder, and her face would pinch in on itself and she'd begin it all over again. Lana spent most of her time laying a hand on her sister-in-law's back and not saying anything. After a handful of breakdowns, Vanessa would glance up at Lana, reminding herself that she was still there, and drape her arms around her neck and cry hot tears onto her shoulder.

"How will we go on, Lana?" she sobbed. "What are we supposed to do?"

Lana whispered empty consoling words, held her and let her cry until she pulled herself away. A part of her wanted to tell

Vanessa about Donnie, about how he wasn't all the way gone yet, like the six-pack in the refrigerator. Hearing of their bedtime conversations may be a comfort to her. But she held back. Vanessa loved her baby brother, had all but raised him single-handedly, and Lana didn't want for her to feel passed over, didn't want to risk turning her grief into anger.

In the end, they inefficiently worked their way into three groupings: that which would stay with Lana, that which Vanessa and her husband Ron would take, and that which would be given away or thrown out. Lana kept the small tools, the things she may need around the house to replace a cracked outlet cover or hang a picture. The heavy tools, Vanessa promised Ron would retrieve one day next week with his pickup truck. At Lana's insistence, Vanessa's backseat was a pile of Donnie's newer clothes, some with the tags still attached, all fortuitously Ron's size. Donnie preferred the tried and true and had to be conned into a new shirt or pair of jeans. The older shirts, Lana kept as night gowns. The older jeans, the ones too worn for Ron to wear to the plant, Lana folded and placed in a black trash bag in the throw out pile. The other keepsakes were divided up evenly based upon the level of emotional attachment. Vanessa tended to the items with dates of origin from Donnie's childhood and Lana took the things from high school on. These things, Lana put into three plastic totes to be hauled into the attic at a later time.

At last, they stood in the driveway, Vanessa having just slammed shut her trunk door on her portion of the things she couldn't bear to see thrown away.

"Van, thanks so much for helping me with this," Lana said as they hugged again. "I never could have done it all without you."

Vanessa pulled back and held Lana's shoulders at an arm's length. She measured Lana with eyes that were red rimmed and puffy. "I believe you could have," she said, her lips quivering a strobe-light smile. "You seem so...," she hesitated, her shaky smile momentarily an image of Donnie's half-face flirty grin. "...*put to-*

gether. You are handling this so much better than I ever..." Then she trailed off into another fit of crying that had them standing there in the driveway holding onto one another for what felt like hours, the summer sun creeping silently toward its hiding place beyond the horizon.

eight

That night, she could hardly wait to tell Donnie all about it. She felt like a soap bubble about to burst. But it was all so much unarticulated emotion and naked abstraction, she didn't yet have the words. So, before going to bed, she decided to force herself to take a warm shower and get her thoughts together.

As the water warmed up in the shower behind her, Lana looked closely at her reflection in the vanity mirror. The sinking sun cast a reddish hue through the small bathroom window, painting her face with nature's makeup. She pulled her hair up and held it behind her head in a ball and leaned in for a closer look. Her cheeks were smooth and rosy, her lips full, her eyes clear, their hazel drawn out by the fading sunlight.

"Put together," she mused to herself.

She thought about Vanessa and her blood-shot eyes and her rubbed-red nose and suddenly she couldn't bear to look at herself. Letting her hair fall to her shoulders, she drew back the shower curtain and stepped in.

Closing her eyes, Lana backed into the spray and the steam and let the water pelt her crown and cascade down where it may. Her hair flowed down her forehead, over her ears, down to where her neck became her shoulders. Her skin grew short-lived goose bumps and she shivered once. The warmth began to loosen muscles she hadn't known were tense. She crossed her arms below her breasts and rolled her upper back into a shepherd's crook. Her head fell forward and her hair washed over her entire face like a mask. The water, like tiny massaging fingers, worked out the kinked knots of fibers in her back that had bunched up while sitting Indian style in the living room floor sorting through Donnie's things.

Donnie.

Donnie was gone. But not all the way gone. Like the beer in the fridge. Or the jeans he only wore to cut the grass, now folded and bagged and awaiting the next garbage pick up.

Lana knew she was going to have to make peace with the idea. To do so, she would have to confront and conquer it. Today was a good first step. She had made herself more nimble, removing items that would weigh her down and make her susceptible to attack. Next, she should prepare an offense, gather stones from the riverbed and untether her sling. The giant was down in the valley awaiting her. She knew the day of their duel was fast approaching, but as she thought about Vanessa, she wasn't sure she was ready. She wasn't even sure if she was ready to *get* ready. No matter her outer appearance. Suddenly, she didn't feel very well *put together* at all. Suddenly, she felt on the very verge of collapse, as if her knees would buckle and she would fold into the corner of the shower, weeping and hugging herself until the water turned ice cold and she was forced to either get up and get out of the shower or die of hypothermia.

But instead, she surprised herself by straightening her spine. In one fluid motion, she swooped her hair back from her face and turned off the water. The sun would be all the way down by now and the prospect of seeing Donnie outmatched her desire to work through her feelings.

She stepped out of the shower and into the relative cool of the room. She dried quickly and wrapped her hair up in a fresh towel. She turned off the overhead fan and through the door, she heard Donnie humming an old country tune she couldn't name and she instantly forgot about everything except slipping into her side of the bed.

nine

The next few days went on much as the last few. Lana would wake early, busy herself around the house for about an hour and then get herself ready and drive to work. The only difference in her morning routine was that she didn't get down Donnie's coffee mug when she got her own and she didn't have to maneuver her Mercury around his big white truck on her way out of the drive. Once she got to the schoolhouse, the tedium of the day would take over and everything would be the same as it always had been. She would work at her computer. She would make copies and sort and file, gather signatures and fax where necessary. Mid-morning, she would unlock the break room and balance out the cash box. She would make her daily run to the post office and re-turn in time to cover for Mr. Darlington's visit to the district office. If a bus driver called in, she would pull out her ancient rolodex and call for a substitute, always finding someone just before the three o'clock line up.

She could do it all with her eyes closed and in a way, she did. Her legs walked her to the correct spots, her fingers typed, her face displayed expressions appropriate for the given situation, but her mind wasn't in the moment. She was chasing butterflies in the meadow of her mind, as Ms. Hale would say, and all the butter-flies and all the meadows led her invariably back to one place and one person.

ten

"Tell that one about your uncle's cow again."

She was laying on her side, her elbow jutted out beneath her pillow, her hand cradling her head. Her other hand played involuntarily with a sprig of her hair that fell across her neck nearly to the mattress. It was an old high school habit that she had forced herself to cease. Donnie had always teased her about it. He would make girly-eyed faces and twirl his own finger in his curly brown hair, raise his voice into a false falsetto and say, "I'm Lana Jones the beauty queen, the prettiest thing you've ever seen." Lana would smile-scowl and hit him on the shoulder with whatever notebook or textbook she had within reach and then they would laugh and go back to whatever they had been arguing about, but with less venom.

Tonight, that old habit had resurfaced, her defenses against it laid down and forgotten. She had gone to bed early, as soon as the sun was down, and they had talked, Lana soaking up every word. The room was darker and if he were still for very long, she had to strain her eyes to see Donnie's profile against the window. In the night sky above them, the moon was but a sliver and nearly new, but their conversation had not waned along with it.

"You've heard that one a million times, Lana-girl," he said. "I bet you could tell it word for word."

She smiled and worked her finger in her hair.

"I could but that's no fun."

Donnie was propped up on both elbows and he let his head rock back for a moment. He groaned as if he didn't want to re-hash that old story, but Lana just waited him out. She knew that it was one of his favorites too, and that once he got rolling on it, he'd enjoy the telling of it as much as she did the hearing.

"That cow liked to kill me and Uncle Sam," he began, same as always and she giggled, same as always. "See," he said playfully, his motor getting cranked up, "you laugh but it wouldn't have been so funny if we hadn't've dropped that old fence gate when we did. You'd've been Poor Little Miss Lana Jones - Girlfriend of Teenage Victim of Murder by Cow for all time. That sort of thing tends to follow a person their whole life. I mean, who would dare to date you much less, marry you for fear of a cow-curse or some-thing? You'd've been an old maid on account of that dad-blamed cow."

Lana laughed through all of this. She still wanted to reach across the bed and pull herself over to him, but it was almost as good just to hear him talk to her like he did way back when. Their laughter died down and she felt he needed a bit of a nudge, so she said, "Just quit your stalling and tell the story already!"

And so he did. He started back at the beginning about how his Uncle Sam had called the house and told Vanessa that he had needed a hand getting an ornery cow into the trailer. Lana liked this version. He was doing his Uncle Sam's voice and everything. It was faint, but she could just make out his hand, its thumb and pinky extended in phone-like fashion beside his face to indicate when he switched from the narrative to their conversation over the telephone.

"So I get dressed and drive on over there," he was saying once he had finished with the preamble. "Uncle Sam's already down at the barn so I walk on down there and when I get there, his back's to me with his hands on his hips and I just figure he's looking out over the pasture. So I stand right up there next to him and put my hands up on my hips, too. Try to look out there and see what he's seeing, kinda like Joshua looking out over Canaan with Moses, you know?"

Lana snickered and said she did. She knew where he was going.

"Well," he continued, "I just happen to look down and I notice that Uncle Sam's not just looking prophetically out over his land. No, ma'am." Donnie shook his head and his curls bounced to and fro. "That old buzzard's got his zipper down and he's using Mother Nature's bathroom right then and there. So of course I take a step or two back, try to get real interested in looking back at the barn or the clouds or my own fingernails or *anything*, but then Uncle Sam - You gotta understand. The man served with the Marines that stormed Iwo Jima. He's seen stuff I can't even imagine. When you go through something like that, I reckon privacy, *especially* your own, ain't much of a concern. - well, Uncle Sam just turns to talk to me, tells me all about this ornery old cow he's trying to load up. All the while, he's just peeing as calmly as you please."

As Donnie went on, Lana stayed in a constant state of joy, at times her laughter spiking to the point of full belly laughs that had them both rolling on the mattress, momentarily unable to continue. But mostly, she just smiled and watched his shadow closely for hand motions and other nonverbal cues that always made the story so much better. Like when he used his balled up fists to simulate the way the cow's big ole eyes looked at the trailer then back at him and the old fence gate he and Uncle Sam were using to goad it along.

"So this cow - this crazy loco heifer - she looks at me and then she looks at the trailer. She takes maybe a step or two toward Uncle Sam's trailer, almost to the point of no return, and then she looks at me one last time and me, I look at her and I can see that behind that big glassy eye, she done made up her mind that she ain't goin' in that trailer. And that's when she did it."

This was when they were juniors at Millwood Branch High and Lana could remember the funny straight-legged way Donnie had walked into school the next morning and the big bloody gauze pads he and Vanessa had taped over the scrapes on his leg. He had tried to hide the injury from the baseball coach because that was the first week of pitchers and catchers that year. After he found out his limp couldn't be hidden, he had told the story to anyone who would listen, embellishing more and more with each iteration. Toward the end of the week, he swore up and down that he had seen his life flash before his eyes looking into that cow's giant glassy one, that an angel had come down from heaven and told him it wasn't his time yet. Lana, to her credit, stood by and only laughed when he did. As it was, he wasn't able to work into his full pitching motion until three or four days before the first game of the season but that was alright for Donnie. He was a natural.

"Ended up pitching some of my best ball that year," he said, resting his head back on his interlocking hands. "God must've known I needed a late start and sent that insane cow to put me outta practice for a couple of weeks."

"You know, some cultures do consider cows to be divine," Lana said, tossing him an easy one just to hear his reaction. But before he responded, he began to turn onto his side away from her. It was almost time for their nightly talk to end. With sadness, Lana realized she could only barely make out the outline of Donnie's shoulder against the window light, his shadow nearly swallowed by that of the room.

"The only divinity about a cow's in how you grill it." He lifted his head once and reset it on his pillow, swooping his hair back as he laid it back down. "And now that you've heard that yarn for the million *and oneth* time, I hope you sleep well my little beauty queen-prettiest thing I've ever seen, with dreams devoid of cattle and old fellers relieving themselves on the ground before you." She couldn't help but let out a schoolgirl's giggle as she allowed her eyelids to drape her vision in total darkness, and not only at what he had said, but also at the fact that he had seen her playing with her hair and had waited until the very end of the night to drop that subtle clue.

That was his way, the small and the subtle, always just enough and never too much. Some girls might've grown tired of it, might've needed more and more as time carried on. Some might've never given it a chance in the first place. Lana loved it. For her, it was always just enough and never too much.

"Good night," she whispered, already half asleep.

The crickets chirping outside and the hum of the central air were all that replied, both playing soft lullabies that carried her away into a night of restfulness.

eleven

The following day was a Saturday and Lana allowed herself to lay in bed as night became dawn and dawn became morning. The sunlight had begun to make golden bars of light on the hardwood as it cut down through the blinds before Lana threw back the covers and sat on the edge of the mattress. She knew that Donnie wouldn't be back come nightfall. The moon would be new. Their gift of time, that gift that is not lightly given, had come to an end.

But it wasn't paralyzing depression that had kept her in bed beyond her normal time this morning. She was sad, yes of course. A part of her, a pretty good chunk, would remain sad forever, she supposed. But around that core of melancholy and sense of loss, she felt a warm presence. All taken, she felt calm and resolute, challenged but capable.

Today, she had decided, would be a good day. She would start it out with a big cup of coffee with extra sugars and milk. Donnie always teased her that she liked what went in coffee better than coffee itself and today, she would prove him true. Her dishes from last night would still be in the sink, so rushed was she to get into bed early last night, so she would follow her coffee with a round of doing the dishes the old fashioned way, washing and drying by hand and putting the things straight away. It always made her feel started out right to have all the dishes in the house clean and done before lunch.

She wouldn't open the lids, she promised herself that. But after the dishes, she would make three trips into the attic, up the fold-down ladder in the hallway, and stack the three plastic totes of Donnie's things in the corner opposite the boxes of Christmas decorations.

That accomplished, she would take a quick shower, just enough to get good and woke up. She decided she would hum something in the shower. Just one song, all the way through, and then she would hop out. One of Donnie's old twangy country tunes would do the trick, maybe *Move It on Over* or *The Bottle Let Me Down*. Memories of both brought a smile to her face. Donnie singing during his after work shower. Donnie singing in his truck, one hand dangling lazily over the steering wheel, the other holding an imaginary microphone.

She'd put on something comfortable, probably jeans and an old t-shirt, lock up, and head out in the Mercury. She thought she would pop in on Vanessa and although she and Ron lived down in Martin and the four-way would be the easiest way to get onto the highway, she would take the cutoff by the old tractor shop. The weather should be beautiful, one of those perfect late summer-early autumn masterpieces, and she would ride with the windows down, her hair pulled back into a ponytail.

She should get to Van and Ron's a little before lunchtime and she wouldn't refuse if they asked her in for a bite. Donnie did their kitchen cabinets a few summers ago as a housewarming gift when they moved to the north side of town and Lana had been his helper on the project as school was out and he joked that he couldn't afford to hire a better hand to help him hang cabinets on a pro bono job. They had made a game out of it and had done as much cutting up as cutting wood. At the end of it, however, Lana had thought that their kitchen was one of Donnie's best. He had, too, bragging more on Lana than himself, but bragging none-the-less.

It would be good for Lana to sit and eat lunch with Vanessa and Ron, swapping small talk about the week behind or the weekend ahead, but it would be even better to sit in their little breakfast nook and look at those kitchen cabinets and remember that summer.

Vanessa would say that she was just about to send Ron up to Millwood Branch in his big Ford to pick up Donnie's tools. Ron would try his best to get her to keep those tools - the large table saw, the miter saw, the drill press, a few others - or offer to help her sell them for profit if she didn't want them taking up space, but she would wave him off and tell him she was sure that Donnie would rather him have them and do with them what he wished. After a few valiant attempts, Ron would relent, and when he did, Lana would suggest them all piling up in his crew cab truck and riding back to her house together. Once they had loaded the power tools, she would ride back to Martin with them and help unload. She would laugh and say that she knew it was silly for her to hitch a ride to her own house and back, especially since her car's already there, but that way they could be all together for the ride. Of course, they would agree - who could deny a grieving widow anything - and after cleaning up after lunch, that's exactly what they would do.

Going through the four-way wouldn't be so bad with company. But she didn't want to go into it unprepared, so she decided that she would be sure to strike up a conversation with Ron about how things were going down at the plant right around when they got to Shop-Rite and not let up until she felt the truck turn and the sun shift and the tires rolling on the smoother blacktop. On the way back, she would turn around in her seat - she knew that her sister-in-law would insist on her sitting shotgun - and ask Van if she remembered the time Donnie had tried to save some money by cutting his own hair. Vanessa would slap her thigh and laugh with her and they would spend the next several minutes telling the story, back and forth between the two of them, about how he couldn't quite get his curls even so he kept snipping them shorter and shorter until finally, he just had to buzz the whole thing off. That had been the week before Senior Prom and Lana had been so mad at the time. After crying over the proofs of their prom pictures, she had made him promise her that he would let it grow until after graduation and that he would never cut it all off again, never ever ever. Donnie had grinned that half faced grin of his and made his vow and stuck out his pinky finger.

That story would get them well past the four-way and maybe nearly to Martin. Before they turned off the highway, Lana would make the suggestion that they should go on into town and grab a milkshake from The Red Bird. Their shakes aren't as good as the Dairy Bar's up in Millwood Branch, but they were alright and it would be her treat for them letting her tag along for the day. Lana would get butterscotch. Vanessa was a constant chocolate and Ron would go with either strawberry or a root beer float. As they sat in the truck waiting for the girl on roller-skates to bring their order, Ron would suggest that maybe they should save some of their ice cream for after supper, that they would make a perfect dessert for the burgers he had planned on grilling that evening.

So they would sip easily on their selections on the way back to Van and Ron's, and place the remainders in their freezer until after the unloading and the grilling and the eating, which they would do out on the back patio, enjoying the perfect temperatures and the beautiful beginning to a stunning sunset.

After the ice cream, Lana would begin saying her goodbyes. There would be warm soft smiles and warm soft hugs and probably a tupperware full of leftover hamburger meat and homemade fries for tomorrow's lunch. She'd probably need her headlights about the time she got up to the old Mill, right about the time she'd be looking for the cutoff to Bullfrog Road, which is easy to miss coming up from the south.

She thought she'd stop at the intersection with Highway 354 and look at their sign, standing at a slant on the corner, the purple spray paint only faded a bit. *D.C. and L.J.*, it said. *Forever*. Dusk would fade into full night, moonless and dark, but she would stay there for a while, her headlights trained on their sign, thinking about the night he had made that promise. *Forever* he had said.

At last, she would drive home, taking the large loop north around town.

She would be tired, but the good kind of tired. She'd place the tupperware in the fridge and help herself to one of his Pabsts and kick off her jeans and change her old t-shirt for one of his. Then she'd crawl into bed and, although she knew he wouldn't be there, she would tell him about the day. She would tell him that she liked his sister and her husband and his cabinetry work and the stories they had created together. She would tell him that she loved him from seventh grade and that she'll love him forever. Then she'd tell him good night and goodbye and she'd turn over and drift slowly into the space between wakefulness and slumber. The room would be so dark that she wouldn't know nor care if her eyes were closed or cracked. The crickets' song would ebb and flow. The big trucks would whir by way out on the highway. The wind would whip around the edge of the house. And from somewhere in the midst of it, she'd almost hear him bid her a good night as well, using her maiden name the way he did, and then she'd fall fast asleep.

Today, she had decided, was going to be a good day. Lana had it all worked out. She looked down at her feet dangling from the edge of the mattress and thought about the little brook behind her momma's house. Thought about how quickly time goes by, especially once it's flowed by you and it's gone. Then she got up and stretched, spreading her arms wide and rising to her tiptoes, the sun warming her back through the window. Lana finished her stretch, her heels thumping on the floor, and turned to make the bed. She undog-eared the sheet and comforter on her side and walked around the footboard. She smoothed a hand over his side and straightened the pillow although it didn't need it. Then she padded into the kitchen and began her day. That big cup of coffee was calling her name.

A Young Man, Once

They say a picture, it's worth a thousand words.

Looking at it, you might not think much. Just a grainy four by six. Some people, a road, a tank. No color save for the unfathomable variations of grey. The people, they are dressed in old and honest clothing. Strapped overalls and work boots, banged up hats made for shade, not for Sunday. Frozen in a time long past. And they are shoulder to grey shoulder in the background, watching without a word. The road, it is shadowed with the crawling of a hundred faint cracks. It runs from God-knows-where to eternity and it is bearing the weight of an army tank, a large white American star painted front and center. The turret is forward-facing, its long cannon is capped and sealed.

There are men perched on the tank, uniformed army men. Two sitting high on the top. They look relaxed, as much as army folk can, as if they are enjoying the ride. Another's face is obscured by the length of the cannon but his arms are visible and crossed lazily over the front of the tank just taking it all in.

And there he is. His head is poked up and profiled from above the star as he drives the monstrous hunk of steel and iron and alloy. He is no bigger than a thumbnail. Face as smooth as a baby's, and though it is difficult to tell for sure, I believe he is grinning as he powers up that pavement by the silent onlookers. He's grinning in that hidden playful way like when he's stolen your nose from your face or he fools you into testing the corn fence and you get a jolt.

He is smiling though, I think he is.

And why shouldn't he? A young man with his whole life laid out before him like a picnic blanket, the road ahead longer than that behind. Why shouldn't a grin play across those youthful lips while the living is good and the world seems pieced back together? It seems only right, a smile does.

His cap is pulled down snug and tight and buckled beneath his chin, goggles laid upon his head and out of the way as he shifts those levers and churns those gov'nment issued treads. His nose is sharp in profile like the edge of a lightning bolt the way he taught me to draw them when my hands were just big enough to wrap clumsily around a crayon. It is the same nose I see in my periphery every time I look down to tie my shoes or button my shirt, the one he passed down to my mother, his daughter, for safekeeping. Until I was ready.

You might not be able to reckon the type of the tank from the picture. I wouldn't. And I am not sure he would remember either, though he might. Names of things were never all too important to him. But he would take his time, pull it apart and grease what needed greasing, tighten what needed another turn. He could get you running again, whatever the name. Then he would likely step back and wipe off his brow and blow air through his lips without a whistle at what man had made.

It's not perfect though, the picture. His hands are absent, missing from it. They are down inside the thing, left and right, unseen and making sure it runs straight and true up that long forgotten roadway. What I wouldn't give to see those hands. Hands that will come to fold over the turning wheel of that ageless brown Chevrolet pick-'em-up, around that morning coffee mug, on the back of that wood-stained pew. His young man hands, no doubt strong enough to do any work that needs doing. No doubt kind enough to handle children and grandchildren, teach them the kindness to handle their own. Strong enough plenty, but kind, like the man they belong to.

And, of course, it could never capture the eyes. Blue refuses to be dealt with on black and white terms and so the pinpoint of his photographed eye remains a mere collection of darkened pixels. Its genuine impact is left to the imagination to color. I see it as I saw it, as everyone who knew him saw. A newborn's blue eyes that never changed. The blue of Saturday skies, of the flag faded on the mast.

Not perfect, no. But a life cannot be passed through a shutter and kept on a film. A man, his essence, all of him, cannot exist wholly within a frame. But reminders can, buoys floating on the endless ocean of time. And this serves as that, as well as any, reminding me of the man he was. Of tractor rides up and down that washboard gravel, of easy chair domino games, and sunburnt backs after potato digging. And a million others that cannot be packaged into words.

But it also speaks of a time before all those. A time when there were some people, a road, and a tank that needed driving. It says that he was a young man, once.

Maybe if he saw it today you would get a chuckle. If you were fortunate, you would get a story, like the one he loved to tell about the time he ran the tracks off a tank during a post-war parade near

White Sands, New Mexico. Maybe he would even slap his knee and say shoot like he would. But I rather think he would just smile. Smile and look. Look with those deep forget-me-not blues that I never have.

A picture, they say, is worth a thousand words. I guess I agree and I guess I don't. Seems such a small price to pay, like the poor widow's two copper mites, for a window into that world, colorless and simple as it may be.

Too small a price, I think.

Story Notes

In my experience, the short story form tends to leave the reader with a lingering desire for more. We become so quickly and completely engrossed in our characters' plights, that we crave more time in their world. Just as we were getting the feel for everything, whammo! It's over. But, but, but! We weren't ready for it to end! There must be more! Such are our minds' demands.

As a writer, this effect can be both gratifying and worrisome. I love to hear readers discuss my stories and I love to hear them pine for more. It lets me know that, even if for only a short time, they were invested enough to complete the journey and, once it was over, to care. Truly, that is all any storyteller could ever hope and dream to achieve. However, there is a fear that the short form would leave readers with a feeling of having been teased, drawn onto an emotional rug just to have it ripped out from under them.

Now, of course, my goal here was to intrigue and fulfill, not dissatisfy; to interest and engage and complete, not to provoke and leave wanting. You, the reader, will be the ultimate judge as to whether or not I have been successful.

In either case, I hope these notes provide you with that "little bit more". I cannot, unfortunately, extend our journey with the characters herein. Although the place in which they exist carries on, the windows through which I peered into their portion of it have been shuttered. Alas, I must leave it to your individual imaginations to write any addendum sections or chapters as you deem necessary.

However, I am convinced new windows will soon open for me, revealing a familiar landscape, perhaps a few well-known faces, as well as a whole slew of new ones. Hopefully, when that time comes, you will be inclined to peek into that world again. Perhaps that peek will become a visit, one in which we can kick our feet up and stay a good while. Until such time, I gladly leave you with these, along with the parting invitation to come on back. You're always welcome here.

Me and Miss Rosie

I began this story with absolutely no intentions of falling senselessly in love with it. At the time, my writings veered toward that which I personally considered to be exciting and attention-grabbing. I placed my characters in situations of immediate peril and prodded them with ever increasing stressors until I discovered whether they would overcome their circumstances or succumb, with more results of the latter category. The faster paced, the better. Shocking, *gruesomely* shocking even - yes! And who could blame me? I was a young, testosterone-driven boy-man and was writing as I would like to read.

Then along came Rosie.

During a brief hiatus from working on my first novel, I made the conscious decision to write something specifically for my wife. Each month, she had dutifully read every chapter of my budding novel (along with every short story that had sprung up during that time period as well) without so much as a whine or a whimper to the fact that those kinds of stories are simply not her thing. Her choicest brand of fiction is that which provokes an entirely different set of emotions than those triggered by the fear of starving to death in the aftermath of an avalanche or the anticipation of an impending escape from a psych ward or the sense of loss after a failed deep space time travel experiment. And so I dialed myself down, took a breather, and wrote the first chapter of what would eventually become this novella.

For a while, I merely tolerated it. The effort required to prevent myself from allowing a sudden alien invasion or mini-nuclear explosion in or around the Bakers' house in Millwood Branch was exhausting. But I enjoyed turning the completed sections over to my wife and watching her become more involved in the story such that it kept me on the correct path. And then somewhere between chapters five and ten (I think) the switch flipped and I *had* to know how Eric Johnston and his new friend ended out. Eric's words flowed easier from then on and the story became increasingly clearer, even to the point of myself becoming a bit weepy once I realized what must happen at its conclusion. Quite a different set of emotions, indeed.

Additionally, I should take this opportunity to point out my most prized moments from this work. The haircutting scene in Miss Rosie's carport is a conglomeration of several childhood memories of my mother cutting mine and my three brothers' hair at our home and is quite special to me. I get a kick out of the fly-by mentions of the Wilbanks twins and the Memphis-based meteorologists and their roles in the changing of the seasons and the passage of time. Lenny Gay was a joy to write. The conversations between Eric and Tiffany were my favorite chapters to put down and remain my favorites to reread. But by far, Rosie Cotcher's spunk, which is channelled directly from my Mamaw and her sisters and is weaved into nearly every corner of this novella, is the reason I absolutely and, as I previously stated, senselessly love this story.

I hope you do, too.

The Traveler

I once asked a well-traveled man what was his most favorite place. He had spent time in Europe, Asia, exotic Caribbean islands, and the entirety of the United States. Without hesitation, he replied, "Gulf Shores, Alabama".

Now, the Alabama gulf coast is extremely nice, without doubt. But his answer took me aback, nonetheless, and challenged me to determine my "best place" as well. This short burst of a story is what became of that thought process as I worked back through our conversation and how I might answer my own question.

This is one of three flash fictions that were originally published in the Dead Mule School of Southern Literature. The other two are compiled here as well. I love the Dead Mule. It is a superb display for stories and authors with a southern slant and I owe them a debt of gratitude for including my works both early and often in my career. If you enjoyed this particular piece, I highly recommend you spend some time perusing the Dead Mule. You're sure to love their stories almost as much as their merchandise, which includes some of the coolest bibs, caps, t-shirts, aprons, and boxer shorts anywhere. Drop them a line, tell them I sent you, and they just might cut you a deal. Or charge you double. Truthfully, it could go either way.

A Sunset for a Suicidist

Every year, Haley and I try our darnedest to spend a few days on the beach. Early in our marriage, before the days of chasing our young'uns across the sand and around the pool, I would find time to hand write a story in an old notebook during the trip.

The first of those stories was a yarn titled, *Compulsion*, which some of you might have had an opportunity to read. The last, thus far, is this story.

Sunset was a rarity as it bloomed in my mind as a completed work - beginning, middle, and end - before I wrote the first word. Typically, I need to meet and get to know my protagonists before I am able to fully determine their ultimate fates. However, and quite unfortunately for her, Belle's course was plotted before I was even wholly settled on her name. Partially owing to the fact that her story was done before it was begun and lacked only me taking it down, and in spite of the depressing nature of its subject matter, it was an extremely enjoyable beach story to write.

This is the second of two stories I have had published in the literary magazine, Bartleby Snopes, the first of which being titled, *Of A Story*. Nathaniel Tower, the managing editor, does an exceptional job of presenting literature of a consistently high quality and I would urge you to explore his magazine and his writings.

Back to the subject of writing on the beach. This is an exercise I would recommend for any writer, novice or experienced. Writing by hand forces a more deliberate and calculated process than that employed by use of a word processor and could possibly both broaden and deepen your understanding of your own voice. Setting a deadline to complete a work, such as, say, before the beach vacation is over, is a great way to gain experience in creating and resolving a conflict in short order. And nothing stokes the creative fire quite like the sound of crashing waves, the warmth of the sun, the cool of the breeze, the shade of a large umbrella, and the view of water without end. So, take my advice. Go to the beach - whichever is closest - and write a story.

What the Storm Did

This one is pretty close to the truth.

Several years ago, a tornado swept through the area where I grew up; my parents' house and my Mamaw's are only separated by a stone's throw (literally). I spent the following day, alongside many friends and family members, cleaning up around Mamaw's. It was quite a memorable day to say the least and it impressed me to the point of writing this little piece which I was fortunate enough to have published by my good friends at the Dead Mule School of Southern Literature.

Two things that I doubt I'll soon forget about that day and that I hope came through in the writing: how quiet and solemn that morning was, and how good-hearted folks band together during such times of tragedy. By that evening, the mood around my grandmother's house had been shifted by the sheer will and power of a community closely knit from that of a funeral to that of a huge family celebration. It was an amazing thing to see and be a part of. I have been so blessed as to have seen it time and time again since and would be willing to bet that I'll see it again.

A word to those affected by storms such as these. Take heart. The destruction of property and materials can be devastating; the sense of utter loss, paralyzing. I understand. But again I say, take heart. If you have your life and the lives of those closest to you, you have that which truly matters. The rest - the trees, the buildings, the *stuff* - will grow again or can be built or bought back. Lean on those around you. Cry on them if you need to. Smile with them when you think you can.

I titled this story *What the Storm Did*. Our storm brought us closer together. I hope yours, if a storm so chooses to sweep through your life, does the same.

From the Backs of
Four Shop-Rite Bags

Remember that "other" set of emotions? The ones fueled by the volatile, combustable male hormone? The ones that yearn for no-escape situations, extreme whiplash-inducing twists and turns, and the likelihood of total and disastrous failure? The ones I had set aside, with effort, to write *Me and Miss Rosie*? Yeah…I pick them back up now and again.

This story originally appeared in a journal by the name of Pantheon Magazine, which produces a fantastic online and print publication, but did not make the initial cut for this collection. Not because I didn't love the story, because I do. And not because I didn't think it was "any count", as my Papaw would say. On the contrary, I found it to be unquestionably entertaining on the low side and an astute character study on the high.

However, at first glance, it just didn't seem to belong. Who would want to read this crazy story about a zombie attack on a small Mississippi town in the midst of all these decidedly non-zombie-esque stories? But, but, but, the other side of my consciousness rebutted, this particular collection *is* based on the *place* and "the zombie story" (as Haley and I had taken to calling it) most assuredly takes place in that place.

While I'll provide no argument to the fact that *Shop-Rite* is indeed an outlier in this collection, in the end, the McBeenes and their quirky yet lovable idiosyncrasies made it impossible for me to exclude it. Maude simply would not have it, the account of her final day ushered to the wayside like the short kid in line at the tilt-a-whirl.

And so, strictly for your enjoyment (oh…and mine), here it is.

As for the rest, this was also a beach story, penciled at some point between *Compulsion* and *Sunset*. I wrote it to answer several questions that were flitting around my mind, the most sophisticated of which was: How would folks from my neck of the woods react to a cataclysmic level event? Would they cut tail and run or hole up somewhere, make good decisions or poor ones? Of course, I also wanted to know more trivial things like whether or not zombies could climb trees and in what song someone like Ole Clutch might lead our trio as they hiked up Muddy Pine Ridge.

Quite unlike *A Sunset for a Suicidist*, I didn't know all the answers when I began writing this one and, luckily, that was just fine. They came easily enough once we got going, Maude, Clutchey, and me.

Goodnight Young Miss Lana Jones

From the very first sentence, *Lana Jones* scared me to my core, scared me to such an extreme that for the longest, I was unable to write further than the first chapter.

The original concept for this story came to me as I was reviewing Eric Johnston's first trip to Miss Rosie's house. If you recall, one of the confounding factors that contributed to his missing the turnoff onto Bullfrog Road was the fact that the road sign had been graffitied by purple spray paint, immortalizing D.C.'s undying love for L.J. I wrote that bit, and the random initials it contains, in a blind flurry devoid of any consideration beyond placing a few flavorful obstacles between Eric and his destination. Sometimes when the words are gushing forth, as they were on that occasion, you run the risk of missing something great if you restrain your inner self with too many questions. It's best if you just let Mr. Hyde do his thing, let him get it all out there on the paper or the screen, and then come back and tidy up later. Sometimes, you might find yourself surprised by what jewels the beast has unearthed. That was the case when I, mild mannered Dr. Jekyll once again, reread the second chapter of *Me and Miss Rosie*. D.C. and L.J. - there was a story behind those letters and it was begging to be told.

So, I concocted this ghostly tale of love and loss to help me bring those letters to life. I had no idea how attached I would become to Lana, Donnie, their forever love, and the situation in which they find themselves until I threw together that first chapter and looked back over it the following morning. That's when the fright set in. No, there's nothing terrifying on the page, my ghost (if you choose to read this story that way) is a friendly one. Embarrassingly, I was scared that I wasn't good enough, that I lacked the ability to properly see L.J. and D.C. through their belated honeymoon. I was afraid of failure. And so that first chapter, of which I was quite proud, sat ignored and unattended to on my hard drive for years.

Meanwhile, I completed *Rosie* and set my sights on presenting her to the world. There needed to be a collection, a body of contributing pieces like backroads that feed into and draw from the main drag. *A Place We All Know* began to come into focus. And suddenly there was no denying that, ready or not, *Lana Jones* must be completed.

Coincidently, around this time, I found myself amidst a brief occupational break, which is a polite way of saying that the store in which I happened to manage a pharmacy closed with little warning and I had not yet secured future employment. I could go on, but I'll spare you. For better or worse, my daytimes were freed up and I had no remaining excuse. At last, I sat down with *Lana* and together we faced our fears and got through those first few trying days after Donnie's funeral.

I don't throw around the term "touching" very often, but I believe it accurately describes how this story is found by me. It hits rather close to home in several different ways. My mother worked as an elementary school secretary for nearly thirty years, beginning on my first day of kindergarten, so Lana's office and daily routine have a solidified place in my consciousness. Furthermore, like Donnie, I discovered my forever love in high school. The backstories and memories that pop up in this story are a combination of my own and others I know well. I do find it touching, and hurtful, but in a good way.

Several folks have asked me how Lana fares after the close of the story. Does the day unfold as she plans? How about the days that follow? Is she going to be "alright"? Of course, I left that to them and, if you have similar questions, I leave it to you. Your Lanas and their next days are likely more interesting to you than mine anyway. However, I will tell you this: I do hope we see her again, somewhere down the road. And until we do, I'll be rooting for her.

A Young Man, Once

Once again, I must thank the good folks at the Dead Mule School of Southern Literature, this time for publishing this piece, my most cherished of the bunch.

A few years after we lost my Papaw, a close friend gave me a framed photograph as a Christmas gift. That photograph is described in these one thousand words. I think it is relatively straightforward, much like the man it is based upon, and does a pretty good job of speaking for itself. Therefore, I won't belabor it with excessive commentary here.

I would, however, like to leave you with this: There is nothing more synonymous with the concept of home than that of family, and the love and support unique to those most basic and irreplaceable of institutions. They come in all different shapes, colors, and sizes. They come with different temperaments, traditions, and values. However yours comes, appreciate it. The members thereof won't be with you forever, so be sure to tell them of your appreciation while you're able. Whether you live close by, as we do, or have distance between you, make your visits as often and as long as possible. You'll all be happier you did.

And that, as we say 'round here, is that.

I invited you along with the notion that you need bring nothing with you, but I hope our time together hasn't left you empty-handed. Every good journey produces a handful of keepsakes and souvenirs. I have mine and I trust you have some of your own. Feel free to show them off during your time away, share with those you brush by on a daily basis. Perhaps they would want to visit this place as well and only needed for you to point them in the right direction. Let them know the front porch light will be on. There'll be something hot in the oven and good folks to enjoy it with. There'll be fellowship and fun, heartbreak and comfort. There'll be laughter and there'll be tears, sometimes both at the same time. There'll be memories shared and memories made.

And stories. There will most definitely be stories.

About the Author

Kevin Winter lives and writes in north Mississippi. His short stories have appeared in numerous online and print publications including Bartleby Snopes, The Medulla Review, Pantheon Magazine, The Battered Suitcase, and The Dead Mule School of Southern Literature. He and his wife, Haley, have two boys, Hudson and Jake, and one rescue dog named Charlie. With his writing, Kevin hopes to highlight the warmth, charm, and uniqueness of his home state and to give back to the place that has given so much to him and his family. Currently, he is marketing his collection of short fiction, *A Place We All Know*, and working on his second novel, *The Two Black Hands of James Carter McMann*, to be set in the compelling world of Hickahala County, Mississippi.

For news and updates on this and other works of Kevin Winter, visit *http://www.facebook.com/kevinwinterwrites*.

Made in the USA
Charleston, SC
12 July 2016